Whispers of Us

SAPPHIC SECOND CHANCES

SAPPHIC SHELLEY

Copyright © 2024 by Sapphic Shelley

All rights reserved.

No part of this book may be reproduced in any form or by any electronic or mechanical means, including information storage and retrieval systems, without written permission from the author, except for the use of brief quotations in a book review.

Introduction

Riley and Morgan stood on the precipice of a new beginning, their love a beacon of hope in the gathering storm. The journey ahead would be fraught with heartache and joy, passion and pain, but together, they vowed silently, they would weather every storm.

The winds of change were blowing through Crescent Bay, and Riley and Morgan's love was about to face its greatest test yet.

The two women, an unlikely pairing of a high school teacher and her former student, had defied the odds once before. Now, as they stared down the barrel of small-town gossip and the disapproval of their families, they clasped hands tighter, knowing that as long as they had each other, they could face anything.

INTRODUCTION

Beneath the surface of friendship lies a deep longing that has persisted through the years. When two women are given a second chance, will they have the strength to turn whispers into a love story?

High school rivals turned best friends, Riley and Morgan, meet again at a reunion in the coastal town of Crescent Bay. For years, both have hidden their true feelings, fueling a tension that has lingered like a secret between them. As the reunion unfolds, old rivalries give way to new revelations, and they must confront the unspoken love that has shaped their lives. With the ocean as their backdrop, can Riley and Morgan finally bridge the gap between friendship and romance, or will past misunderstandings drown their chance at happiness?

One

RILEY STEPPED into the elegantly decorated banquet hall, her emerald green dress swishing softly against her legs. She paused for a moment, breathless, taking in the shimmering fairy lights draped along the walls, the lush floral centerpieces adorning each table, the lively chatter and laughter echoing through the space. The air hummed with excitement and nostalgia, thick with the layered scents of perfume and memories.

Riley's fingers tightened around her sequined clutch. They had to be here somewhere. Sam had texted her just an hour ago, gushing that she couldn't wait to see her. Unless—a flicker of doubt crept into Riley's mind—something had changed?

She stepped forward, her heels clicking on the

gleaming floor. Weaving through the throngs of people, fragments of conversation floated by.

"Has it really been ten years since—"

"—still looks incredible, like no time has passed—"

"—remember sneaking out to—"

The echoes of the past called to Riley, but she pushed them aside. Find her friends now. Reminisce later. Scanning the room, she maneuvered between groups of old classmates, whispering "excuse me" as she passed.

Then, as if the sun had emerged from behind the clouds, she saw them by the bar. Ethan's wild curls. Lily's glittery top catching the light. The strong line of Sam's shoulders. Riley's face broke into a huge smile, joy radiating through her.

She was home.

* * *

Riley charged through the crowded room, her eyes locked on Sam. As she drew near, Sam spun around, her face splitting into a huge grin. They crashed into each other's arms, hugging fiercely, their bond as strong as ever.

"Riles!" Sam cried, her voice muffled against Riley's shoulder. "Fuck, it's been too long!"

Riley laughed, a burst of pure joy. She squeezed Sam tighter, inhaling the familiar scent of her vanilla perfume. "Way too long, Sammy. God, I've missed you."

Stepping back, they clasped hands, drinking each other in. Sam looked radiant, her red hair falling in soft waves, her smile warm and inviting. Riley's heart filled with affection, the years melting away until it felt like they'd never been apart.

"Damn, girl," Sam said, her eyes sparkling mischievously. "You're looking fine as hell, Riles."

Riley ducked her head, feeling a blush creep up her neck. "Shut up, you're making me go all red."

"Just calling it like I see it," Sam grinned, giving Riley's hands a firm squeeze. "Seriously though, I'm so fucking proud of you. You've accomplished so much, become this incredible person... it's mind-blowing."

Riley's throat tightened, Sam's sincere words hitting her right in the gut. She blinked back tears, swallowing hard. "I couldn't have done it without you, Sam. You've always been there for me, through thick and thin."

Sam's smile softened, her eyes glistening with emotion. "And I always will be. That's a promise."

For a moment, they stood hand in hand, the world around them disappearing. Riley's heart swelled with gratitude for Sam's unwavering support and love over the years. Their friendship was a force of nature, unbreakable and true.

Yet even as she reveled in their reunion, Riley couldn't shake the nagging thoughts of her unfinished business with Morgan, the unanswered questions lingering like a dark cloud. In her heart, she knew she had to confront the past to truly move forward.

But for now, she allowed herself to be swept up in the joy of being with Sam, letting their reunion push everything else to the background. The ghosts of her past could wait. In this moment, surrounded by the people she loved most, Riley was exactly where she needed to be.

* * *

Across the room, Riley's gaze locked onto a familiar figure, causing her breath to catch in her throat. Morgan Hughes, the girl who could set Riley's heart racing and palms sweating with a mere glance.

Their eyes briefly connected, a spark of recognition flickering between them before Morgan quickly averted her gaze, her expression inscrutable.

Riley's heart thundered in her chest as she watched Morgan navigate through a group of their old classmates, her laughter rising above the chatter filling the room. She was a vision of effortless beauty, her golden hair shimmering beneath the gentle lights, her sapphire eyes twinkling with amusement. It seemed as though time had stood still, yet everything had irrevocably shifted.

Conflicting emotions surged through Riley as she wrestled with her next step. A part of her yearned to bridge the gap between them, to finally confront the unspoken feelings that had long simmered just beneath the surface. Yet, another part held her back, fear and uncertainty twisting in her gut like a coiled serpent poised to attack.

Should I approach her? Riley pondered, worrying her lip as she observed Morgan tilt her head back, laughing heartily at a classmate's comment.

What would I even say? 'Hey, remember me? The girl you despised in high school? Feel like catching up?'

She mentally shook herself, attempting to banish the doubts clouding her thoughts. This was her opportunity, possibly her sole chance, to make things right between them. To lay the past to rest and move ahead, unburdened by the weight of their shared history. Still, she wavered, her feet seemingly cemented in place by an unseen force.

The reunion carried on around her, oblivious to the internal battle raging within. Laughter and conversation swirled in the air, intertwining with the gentle melodies emanating from the speakers.

Come on, Riley, she silently admonished herself, drawing a steadying breath. *You've got this. Just walk over and say hello. What's the worst that could happen?*

Yet, even as she mustered her resolve, Riley understood that the answer to that question was far more complex than she wished to acknowledge. Because with

Morgan, nothing was ever straightforward. And the worst that could happen? Well, that was a gamble she wasn't certain she was prepared to take.

Two

RILEY GUIDED Morgan onto the dance floor, the touch of her hand igniting a spark within Morgan's core. They navigated through the sea of swaying couples until they found their own little island, just as a slow, romantic melody began to play. Riley turned to face Morgan, her emerald eyes glistening with a cocktail of nerves and anticipation.

Morgan inched closer, hands settling on Riley's waist as Riley's arms draped around her neck. They fell into a rhythm, their bodies moving as one, as if they'd never skipped a beat. Morgan inhaled deeply, taking in Riley's signature scent—a captivating blend of jasmine and the ocean breeze that always clung to her skin.

Morgan's eyes drifted to Riley's lips, lingering for a heartbeat before she caught herself and glanced away, a rosy flush spreading across her cheeks. "I'm really glad you came," she said softly, her voice intimate. "There's so much I've been wanting to say to you, to try and make things right between us."

Riley's pulse quickened at the unspoken promise in those words, the thrilling possibility that her long-held feelings might not be one-sided after all. "Me too," she confessed, her voice catching slightly. "You have no idea how much."

They stood in silence for a long moment, the reunion fading into the background as they lost themselves in each other's gaze. Morgan finally spoke, a hint of nervousness in her tone. "Do you remember the day I left for college? The last time we saw each other?"

Riley's breath caught at the memory, the phantom touch of Morgan's lips grazing her cheek in a goodbye that had felt like both a beginning and an end. "How could I forget?" she murmured, aching to reach out and caress Morgan's face, to feel the warmth of her skin beneath her fingertips.

Morgan's eyes shimmered with a swirl of emotions - longing, regret, and something deeper that Riley couldn't quite put her finger on. "I wanted to kiss you that day," she admitted, her voice barely above a whisper. "I wanted to tell you how I really felt, how I'd always felt. But I was too afraid. Afraid of what it meant, of what everyone would think. Afraid of losing you."

Riley's eyes widened, her heart skipping a beat as the truth of their shared past clicked into place. "I wanted that too," she breathed, emotion thickening her voice. "I wanted you, Morgan. I always have. But I didn't know how to tell you, how to get you to see it..."

Her words trailed off, lost in the magnetic pull of Morgan's eyes, the electric tension crackling between them. And then, throwing caution to the wind, Riley closed the distance and captured Morgan's lips with her own in a kiss that was both tender and fiercely passionate.

As their mouths met, a jolt of desire raced down Riley's spine, igniting the long-buried hunger that had smoldered within her for years. Morgan's lips were velvety soft, melding perfectly with hers as if they were always meant to be together. Everything else melted away, leaving only the press of Morgan's curves against her own, the intoxicating taste of her, the heady scent of her perfume filling Riley's senses.

When they finally pulled apart, both women were flushed and breathless, their eyes bright with wonder and want. Riley laughed softly, giddy with a happiness she'd never known. "I can't believe this is really happening," she marveled, her fingers threading through Morgan's silky hair. "I've fantasized about this for so long, but I never imagined..."

Morgan cut her off with another searing kiss, slower and more sensual. "I know," she breathed against Riley's lips. "I never thought I'd be brave enough to admit how I felt. But seeing you tonight, being with you like this... it just feels so right."

They held each other close, foreheads touching, savoring the closeness they'd both craved for so long. The reunion carried on around them, their old classmates' voices fading into the background as they lost themselves in each other.

"God, I've missed this," Riley breathed, her words tickling Morgan's ear. "I've missed you, Morgan."

Morgan's heart stumbled at the raw vulnerability in Riley's voice. "I've missed you too, Riles," she murmured, fingers digging into Riley's hips. "You have no idea how much."

As they swayed, the world around them faded away, leaving just the two of them, suspended in a moment that felt both thrillingly new and hauntingly familiar. Morgan allowed herself to get lost in the sensation of Riley's body against hers, their heartbeats synchronizing with each step.

But even as she melted into the moment, a nagging whisper in the back of her mind served as a bitter reminder. This was temporary, it cautioned her. They'd been down this road before, and it had only led to shattered hearts. What was different this time?

Riley drew back slightly, as if attuned to her thoughts. "Hey, what's on your mind?" she asked gently, fingers absently toying with the wispy hairs at the nape of Morgan's neck.

Morgan wavered, caught between the urge to be truthful and the fear of shattering this fragile moment. "I'm thinking about how badly I want this," she confessed, her voice scarcely audible. "But I'm also remembering how much it hurt when it fell apart last time. I don't know if I can handle that again, Riles."

Riley's eyes melted, her hand drifting up to cradle Morgan's cheek. "I know, babe," she whispered, thumb grazing Morgan's skin. "But we've both grown since then. We're not the same people we used to be. Maybe...maybe this time, things could be different."

Morgan nestled into Riley's touch, eyes drifting shut for a heartbeat. Every fiber of her being yearned to believe that, to dive headfirst and see where this could lead. But the fear persisted, a leaden knot in her gut.

"I don't know," she breathed, eyes fluttering open to lock with Riley's once more. "I just...I need some time to process this. To figure out if I'm ready to take this leap."

Riley nodded, a flicker of disappointment ghosting across her features before she concealed it with an understanding smile. "Of course," she said softly, hand falling away from Morgan's cheek. "Take all the time you need, Morgan. I'll be here, whenever you're ready."

As the final notes of the song faded away and they reluctantly disentangled, Morgan found herself awash in a tempest of clashing emotions—hope and fear, longing and hesitation, all churning together in a dizzying whirlwind. She knew this was merely the beginning, that there was so much left unwritten. But for now, all she could do was draw in a steadying breath and step off the dance floor, her heart brimming with possibilities and her mind awhirl with questions that only time held the answers to.

"Want to get out of here?" Riley asked abruptly, her voice husky with need. "We could find somewhere private, somewhere we can really talk... or not talk." She smirked, her eyes twinkling playfully.

Morgan giggled, the sound pure music to Riley's ears. "Hell yes," she purred, intertwining their fingers and pulling Riley toward the door. "You lead, Thompson. I'm all yours tonight."

As they escaped into the crisp evening air, Riley marveled at how the night had unfolded. She'd come to the reunion hoping for closure, a chance to finally put the past to rest. Instead, she'd discovered something far more precious - a second chance at love, a future full of endless possibility.

And as she strolled hand-in-hand with Morgan under the starry sky, Riley knew that no matter what challenges tomorrow might bring, they would weather them together, their love strong enough to overcome anything.

Three

RILEY LEANED CLOSE, her shoulder grazing Morgan's as a mischievous smile played on her lips. "Hey, what do you think about taking a walk on the beach, just you and me?"

Morgan paused, catching her bottom lip between her teeth as conflicting emotions flickered across her face. Uncertainty, yearning, a hint of apprehension... But beneath it all, an undeniable spark of desire.

"Alright," Morgan finally breathed, her gaze locking with Riley's, a newfound intensity burning in her eyes. "I'm in."

Riley drew in a deep breath, the briny scent of the ocean filling her lungs as the distant crash of waves reached her ears. The tension in her muscles began to ease, and beside her, Morgan shuddered slightly in the cool evening air. Riley's fingers itched to reach out and pull her close, to share her warmth, but she resisted the temptation.

They strolled along the boardwalk in electric silence, their steps falling into sync. Riley couldn't help but steal a glance at Morgan, admiring the graceful angles of her profile, the way the moonlight danced across her skin. Questions raced through her mind, but she swallowed them back, savoring the sweet torture of anticipation.

"So," Morgan's voice cut through the quiet, shattering the moment. "Catch me up. What's been going on with you since... Well, since the last time we saw each other?"

Her words faltered slightly, and Riley's heart squeezed painfully. The memories of their previous encounter lingered between them, a poignant mix of regret and unfulfilled potential.

But as Riley opened up, the stories tumbling from her lips in a cleansing flood, the burden of the past seemed to lift. She shared her triumphs and struggles with her business, the exhilaration and disappointments that came with pursuing her ambitions. Morgan, in turn, spoke of her writing journey, the electrifying high of seeing her name in print, the relentless whisper of self-doubt that lurked in the shadows.

With each step, each intimate revelation, Riley sensed the bond between them growing stronger, more tangible. It was as though the years had melted away, and yet, everything was different. The innocent, naive girls they had once been had blossomed into intricate, captivating women, their experiences and scars only serving to draw them nearer.

As they turned a corner, Riley spied a weathered bench hewn from driftwood and impulsively pulled Morgan towards it. They settled onto the sun-warmed surface, their bodies pressed together from shoulder to thigh, Morgan's heat seeping through the thin fabric of Riley's dress.

"I'm so glad you're here," Riley murmured, the confession slipping out before she could reconsider. "Being with you again... It just feels right. Like coming home."

She held her breath, her pulse pounding in her ears as she awaited Morgan's reaction. The other woman was quiet for a long moment, her gaze fixed on the restless swell of the waves. Then, slowly, she turned to face Riley, their faces mere inches apart.

"I know what you mean," Morgan whispered, her breath warm against Riley's lips. "I've been running for so long, searching for something I couldn't quite put my finger on. But now... Now I think I've finally found it."

Riley's throat tightened, lost in the fathomless depths of Morgan's eyes. The space between them crackled with electricity, with the aching need and barely restrained passion of years gone by. She longed to bridge the gap, to claim Morgan's lips with her own and unleash the feelings she'd kept locked away for an eternity.

But a flicker of doubt held her back. After all this time, all the words left unspoken and opportunities squandered, Riley was petrified of shattering this delicate, flawless moment...

Riley's heart thundered in her chest as she met Morgan's unwavering gaze, the crashing surf fading into the background. The sinking sun enveloped them in a warm, amber embrace, shadows playing across the contours of Morgan's face. Riley's fingers twitched, aching to reach out and trace the soft curve of her cheek, to lose themselves in the silken strands of her hair.

"Morgan, I..." Riley began, her voice quivering slightly. She inhaled deeply, summoning her courage. "I never stopped thinking about you. About us, and what we could have had."

Morgan's eyes grew wide, a glimmer of surprise and something deeper, more profound, flickering across her features. She reached out, her fingertips grazing Riley's hand, igniting a trail of sparks along her skin.

"I thought it was just me," Morgan admitted softly, her thumb tracing gentle circles on Riley's flesh. "I told myself you must have moved on, that I'd lost my chance."

Riley shook her head, a quiet, incredulous laugh escaping her throat. "How could I ever move on from you? You're the one I've always wanted, Morgan. The one I've always needed."

The words hung heavy in the air, laden with promise

and possibility. Morgan's hand glided up Riley's arm, leaving a wake of goosebumps in its path. She cradled Riley's face, her touch tender and reverent.

"I'm here now," Morgan breathed, her eyes searching Riley's. "And I'm not going anywhere. Not this time."

Riley's breath hitched, her heart swelling with an overwhelming, fierce joy. She leaned in, erasing the final distance between them, and captured Morgan's lips in a soft, lingering kiss.

It was a kiss that spoke of years of yearning, of countless fantasies and dreams finally realized. Morgan's lips were soft and warm, moving against Riley's with a gentle urgency that made her head reel. She tangled her fingers in Morgan's hair, drawing her closer, deepening the kiss until they were both left breathless.

When they finally broke apart, foreheads touching, Riley couldn't suppress the giddy laughter that bubbled up from her chest. Morgan's eyes danced with a happiness Riley had never witnessed before, and she couldn't help but join in.

Morgan reached out, her fingers grazing Riley's cheek with a gentle touch. "Hey, failure happens to everyone," she said, her blue eyes filled with understanding. "But it's also a chance to learn and become stronger. And you, Riley Thompson, are the toughest, most resilient person I know. You've got what it takes to overcome anything and chase your dreams, no matter how scary they might seem."

Riley leaned into Morgan's touch, her eyes closing as a tear slipped down her cheek. "I'm terrified," she admitted, her voice barely audible. "Terrified of the unknown, of leaving behind everything I've worked so hard for."

Morgan wiped the tear away with her thumb, her touch comforting and reassuring. "I get it," she said softly, her own voice wavering with emotion. "I've been scared too, scared of opening up and getting hurt. But being here with you, sharing my fears and vulnerabilities, it's made me realize that some risks are worth taking."

Riley opened her eyes, locking gazes with Morgan. In those blue depths, she saw the same vulnerability, the same yearning for a deeper connection. In that moment, the world around them disappeared, leaving only the two of them and the unspoken words hanging between them.

"Morgan," Riley breathed, her heart racing. "I..."

Before she could finish, Morgan leaned in, her lips meeting Riley's in a soft, tentative kiss. Riley's breath hitched, electricity coursing through her body as she melted into the kiss, her hands reaching up to tangle in Morgan's silky blonde hair.

When they finally pulled apart, both women were breathless, their cheeks flushed and their eyes shining with newfound understanding. The world seemed brighter somehow, the colors more vivid, the sounds more alive.

"We should probably head back," Riley murmured

reluctantly, her fingers playing with the collar of Morgan's shirt. "Before they send out a search party."

Morgan grinned, pressing a quick, playful kiss to the corner of Riley's mouth. "Let them wait," she teased, her voice low and husky. "I've waited long enough for this moment. For you."

Riley's heart soared, love and desire washing over her. She captured Morgan's lips in another searing kiss, pouring all the unspoken words and pent-up emotions into the embrace.

Riley and Morgan lost themselves in each other, their laughter and sighs mingling with the whisper of the waves. It was a moment of pure, perfect happiness, a promise of all the love and adventures to come.

Riley's eyes sparkled as she turned to Morgan, her voice soft and inviting. "Why don't we sit for a bit? I'm not quite ready to head back yet."

Morgan nodded, a small smile playing at the corners of her lips. "I'd like that."

They settled onto a nearby driftwood log, the weathered wood smooth beneath their hands. Riley's shoulder brushed against Morgan's, sending a thrill through her body. The air between them felt charged, heavy with unspoken desires and hidden longings.

Riley's heart raced as she glanced at Morgan, her eyes tracing the elegant lines of her profile. The golden light of the setting sun cast a warm glow over Morgan's features, highlighting the flecks of gold in her hazel eyes and the soft curve of her lips. Riley's breath caught, overwhelmed by the sudden surge of emotion.

Morgan turned, catching Riley's gaze. Her eyes searched Riley's face, a silent question hanging between them. Riley swallowed hard, her mouth suddenly dry. She wanted to reach out, to touch Morgan's face, to run her fingers through her silky hair. But she hesitated, uncertainty holding her back.

"Riley," Morgan breathed, her voice barely above a whisper. "I..."

But before she could finish, Riley leaned in, closing the distance between them. Their lips met in a soft, tentative kiss, a gentle exploration of the feelings that had been building all evening. Morgan's hand came up to cup Riley's cheek, her fingers warm and gentle against Riley's skin.

The world around them faded away, narrowing down to just the two of them and the intensity of their connection. Riley's heart pounded, a heady mix of excitement and nervousness coursing through her veins. She deepened the kiss, her tongue brushing against Morgan's in a tantalizing dance.

Morgan let out a soft moan, her fingers tangling in Riley's hair. She pulled Riley closer, their bodies pressing together as the kiss grew more heated. Riley's hands roamed over Morgan's back, mapping the contours of her body through the thin fabric of her dress.

Time seemed to stand still as they lost themselves in each other, the sound of the waves and the distant chatter of the reunion fading into the background. Riley's mind spun with the possibilities of what this moment could mean, of the future that stretched out before them.

Finally, they broke apart, both breathless and flushed. Morgan rested her forehead against Riley's, a shy smile playing at the corners of her mouth.

"That was..." she murmured, her voice husky.

"Incredible," Riley finished, her own smile mirroring Morgan's.

They sat in comfortable silence for a moment, their fingers intertwined as they watched the last rays of sunlight disappear below the horizon. The air grew cooler, the breeze carrying the briny scent of the sea.

"We should probably head back," Morgan said reluctantly, her thumb tracing circles on the back of Riley's hand.

Riley nodded, a small sigh escaping her lips. "Probably," she agreed, though she made no move to stand up.

Morgan chuckled, a playful glint in her eye as she leaned in and pressed a soft kiss to Riley's temple. "Come on, you," she teased, her fingers intertwining with Riley's as she tugged her gently to her feet. "We've got the rest of our lives to sit here and be sappy. Let's go make the most of tonight."

Riley grinned, her heart soaring as she allowed Morgan to pull her up and into a tight embrace. They held each other close, savoring the warmth and comfort of finally being together after so many years of missed chances and unspoken feelings.

* * *

Hand in hand, they made their way back towards the reunion, their steps falling into a perfect rhythm as if they'd been walking side by side all their lives. The future stretched out before them, full of endless possibilities and the promise of a love that had stood the test of time.

As they approached the glowing lights of the venue, Morgan suddenly stopped, turning to face Riley with an intensity that made her breath catch in her throat. "Riley, before we go back in there, I need you to know something," she said softly, her voice trembling with emotion. "This thing between us, it's not just some fleeting reunion hookup or a trip down memory lane. It's real, and it's powerful, and it's..."

"Everything," Riley finished for her, her eyes shining with the depth of her feelings. "It's everything I've ever wanted, Morgan. Everything I never knew I needed until I found you again."

Morgan's face broke into a radiant smile, tears of joy glistening in her eyes as she leaned in and captured Riley's lips in a searing kiss that left them both breathless and weak in the knees. They melted into each other's arms, the rest of the world falling away until there was nothing left but the two of them and the love that burned between them.

When they finally broke apart, flushed and giddy with happiness, Riley knew without a doubt that this was just the beginning of their forever.

Stepping back into the reunion hand in hand, Riley couldn't keep the grin off her face as they wove their way through the crowded room. The air hummed with laughter and chatter, the warm glow of the chandeliers casting a romantic light over everything. Out of the corner of her eye, she caught a glimpse of their reflection in an ornate mirror and felt her heart skip a beat at the sight of them together, radiant and so clearly in love.

"Well, well, well, look who finally decided to grace us with their presence!" a familiar voice called out teasingly, and they turned to see Samantha, an old friend, waving at them from across the room with a knowing smirk. "And just where have you two been all night, hmm?"

Riley glanced at Morgan, a mischievous glint in her eye as she wrapped an arm around her waist and pulled her close. "Oh, you know, just catching up on old times," she replied airily, her voice dripping with innuendo.

"Lots and lots of catching up," Morgan added with a wink, her hand finding Riley's and giving it a conspiratorial squeeze.

As they rejoined their friends, falling easily into the laughter and reminiscing, Riley marveled at how natural it felt to be with Morgan like this, trading secret smiles and flirtatious touches like they'd been doing it all their lives. It was as if every moment, every choice, every twist and turn in their separate paths had been leading them right here, right to each other.

* * *

They danced the night away in each other's arms, lost in their own little world as the rest of the reunion carried on around them. And later, as the crowd began to thin and the music turned slow and sweet, Riley pulled Morgan close and whispered in her ear, "Let's get out of here, just you and me."

Morgan shivered at the heat in her voice, her eyes darkening with desire as she nodded and laced their fingers together. "Lead the way," she murmured, a wicked smile playing at the corners of her mouth.

Hand in hand, they slipped out of the reunion and into the cool, star-studded night, their hearts racing with anticipation and the thrill of new beginnings. The future was theirs for the taking, and with Morgan by her side, Riley knew that anything was possible. This was their second chance, their fresh start, and she was going to make damn sure they made the most of every single moment.

Four

THE FLAMES of the bonfire danced and crackled, casting a warm glow on the faces of Riley and Morgan's former classmates as they approached the gathering on the beach. The familiar scent of salt air and burning wood filled their nostrils, bringing back memories of a simpler time. Friendly voices called out to greet them, welcoming them back into the fold.

"Well, well, look who decided to grace us with their presence!" a voice teased good-naturedly. "I thought you two had forgotten all about us!"

Riley grinned, her eyes twinkling with amusement. "Please, as if we could ever forget this motley crew. Besides, someone has to keep you all in line."

Morgan chuckled, shaking her head as she took in the scene. It was surreal being back here, surrounded by the people and places of their youth. A part of her had thought she'd left this all behind, but the pull of nostalgia was stronger than she'd anticipated.

As they settled into the circle of friends, the banter and laughter flowed effortlessly, old stories and inside jokes resurfacing like long-lost treasures. For a moment, it was as if no time had passed at all, and they were all carefree teenagers once more.

But as the night wore on, Riley found herself yearning for a moment alone with Morgan. Catching her eye across the flickering flames, she tilted her head towards the shoreline, a silent invitation. Morgan nodded, and they quietly slipped away from the group, their absence hardly noticed amidst the merriment.

The cool sand felt refreshing beneath their feet as they walked along the water's edge, the rhythmic crash of the waves a soothing backdrop to their thoughts. The moon hung low in the sky, painting the ocean in shimmering silver.

"Feels a bit surreal, doesn't it?" Riley mused, her voice soft against the night air. "Being back here, after all this time..."

Morgan hummed in agreement, her gaze fixed on the distant horizon. "Yeah, it's like we've stepped into a time warp or something. Everything's so familiar, but at the same time, it feels like a lifetime ago."

Riley paused, a flicker of uncertainty crossing her

features. "Hey, can I tell you something?" she asked, turning to face Morgan.

"Of course, you can tell me anything," Morgan replied, her tone gentle and reassuring.

"It's just... sometimes I wonder if I've actually made anything of myself since we left this place," Riley confessed, the words tumbling out in a rush. "Like, have I really grown or changed, or am I just stuck in the same old rut?"

Morgan reached out, taking Riley's hand in a comforting squeeze. "Are you kidding? Look at everything you've achieved, Riles. You built a successful business from the ground up, you've traveled the world... that's not nothing."

Riley leaned into the touch, drawing strength from Morgan's unwavering support. "I know, I know. But sometimes the doubts just creep in, you know? Like I'm waiting for the rug to be pulled out from under me."

"That's just the human condition, babe," Morgan said with a wry smile. "We all feel that way sometimes. But you've got this. And you've got me, always."

Riley felt a warmth bloom in her chest, the weight of her fears slowly dissipating. There was something about Morgan's steady presence that made everything feel more manageable, more hopeful.

That night, due to the lack of total privacy, camping

went the reunion group on the beach, Riley and Morgan held each other close beneath their shared blankets and longed for the reunion party to end.

* * *

Unable to discretelly the control their passion, and sensing the prying eyes on them, Riley and Morgan rose, strolled along the shore, the cool sand cushioned their bare feet with each step. The distant bonfire cast a warm, flickering glow across their faces, illuminating their features in a mesmerizing dance of light and shadow. Riley's heart skipped a beat as she felt the tantalizing brush of Morgan's hand against her own, a subtle yet electrifying touch that ignited a spark within her.

Their conversation took a more introspective turn as they wandered further from the crowd. Morgan spoke passionately about her dream of becoming a successful author, her voice brimming with quiet determination that Riley couldn't help but admire. She recounted the challenges she'd faced in the ruthless publishing industry, the rejections and setbacks that had only strengthened her resolve to make it.

Riley found herself captivated by Morgan's words, drawn in by the depth of her passion and the sharp intellect that shone in her eyes. In return, Riley shared her own aspirations and the doubts that sometimes crept in as she navigated the trials of entrepreneurship.

"I've always admired your resilience," Morgan said softly, her gaze locking with Riley's under the moonlight. "The way you keep pushing forward, no matter what life throws at you."

Riley felt a warm flush at the compliment, a smile tugging at her lips. "It's not always been a smooth ride," she confessed, her voice barely above a whisper. "But I've learned that the biggest payoffs often come from pushing through the toughest times."

As they walked, their hands continued to graze against each other, each fleeting touch sending a jolt of electricity through Riley's body. She yearned to intertwine her fingers with Morgan's, to feel the comforting warmth of her hand in her own.

The air between them grew thick with unspoken desire, the tension evident in every stolen glance and lingering touch. Riley's heart raced as she realized her feelings for Morgan had grown far beyond simple friendship.

In that moment, walking along the moonlit shore, Riley knew she was on the brink of something both thrilling and terrifying. The possibility of a future with Morgan, of exploring the depths of their connection, filled her with a dizzying mix of excitement and nerves.

As they turned back towards the bonfire, Riley

savored the feeling of Morgan's hand in her own, the promise of what lay ahead hanging in the salty air between them. Whatever the future held, she knew this moment, this connection, would be forever seared into her memory.

Five

THE MORNING SUN peeked through the coastal fog, illuminating the campsite with a soft glow. Riley crawled out of her tent, hair a mess and eyes still half-closed. She stretched, yawning, and spotted Morgan already up and about, getting ready for their hike.

"Well, look who decided to join the land of the living," Morgan quipped, flashing Riley a playful grin. "You ready to hit the trails, sleepyhead?"

Riley couldn't help but smile, Morgan's teasing instantly perking her up. "Oh, I was born ready," she shot back, matching Morgan's energy. "Been counting down the days 'til this hike since we planned the reunion."

The group gathered their gear, shouldering backpacks and double-checking their hiking boots. As they set off,

Riley and Morgan naturally fell into step beside each other, their rhythm in sync.

The trail led them through a lush forest of towering pines and vibrant ferns, the earthy scent of damp soil and pine needles filling the air. Birdsong mingled with the distant roar of the ocean, a natural symphony.

"Hey, remember when we got lost on that nature reserve field trip back in high school?" Riley asked, a mischievous twinkle in her eye.

Morgan burst out laughing. "God, how could I forget? We found that hidden waterfall and just spent the whole day swimming and goofing off."

"Meanwhile, everyone else was losing their minds trying to find us," Riley added, grinning at the memory.

As they tackled a steep incline, Riley felt Morgan's hand on her lower back, a silent gesture of support. The touch sent a jolt through her, and she found herself leaning into it, wanting more.

They reached a clearing overlooking the vast ocean. The salty wind whipped through their hair as Riley closed her eyes, savoring the moment. When she opened them, she caught Morgan watching her, an unreadable expression on her face.

"What's on your mind?" Riley asked softly, curious.

Morgan hesitated, glancing down before meeting Riley's gaze. "Just... how much I've missed this," she admitted, her voice thick with emotion. "Being here with you, it feels like home."

Riley's heart swelled at Morgan's words. She reached out, her fingers grazing Morgan's, a silent acknowledgment of their shared feeling.

Standing there, the world narrowed to just the two of them, their connection growing stronger with each heartbeat. The future stretched out before them, full of promise and possibility, and Riley knew that whatever happened, she wanted Morgan by her side.

"It's funny," Riley mused, her voice soft and reflective. "I never thought I'd find myself back here, in Crescent Bay, with you by my side."

Their eyes met, and in that moment, a thousand unspoken words passed between them. Morgan's gaze held a depth of emotion that took Riley's breath away, a longing that had been simmering since that fateful night by the bonfire. The pull between them was undeniable, a force that drew them together like the moon pulling the tides.

Riley's heart raced as she leaned in, the distance between them vanishing with each passing second. Is this what it feels like to fall head over heels for someone?

Morgan's breath caught in her throat, her eyes darting to Riley's lips. The tension between them was palpable, the air crackling with electricity. And then, as if by some unspoken agreement, their lips crashed together in a searing kiss.

The world fell away, leaving only the sensation of soft lips moving in perfect harmony, hands gently cradling faces, and hearts beating as one. The kiss was a revelation, a moment of pure, unadulterated joy that seemed to last a lifetime.

When they finally broke apart, breathless and flushed, Riley couldn't help but marvel at the way Morgan's eyes sparkled in the fading light. In that moment, she knew with absolute certainty that this was just the beginning of something incredible.

A smile played across Riley's lips as she gazed at Morgan, her heart soaring with newfound happiness. The kiss had ignited a fire within her, a warmth that spread from head to toe, leaving her giddy with excitement.

"That was..." Riley started, her voice barely above a whisper.

"Pretty damn amazing," Morgan finished, her eyes shining with a mix of wonder and affection. She gave Riley's hand a gentle squeeze, a silent confirmation of the bond they shared.

As they continued their hike, the forest seemed to come alive around them. The gentle rustling of leaves, the melodic birdsong, and the distant crash of waves against the shore created a perfect backdrop for their blossoming romance.

Riley couldn't help but sneak glances at Morgan as they walked, admiring the way the golden light illuminated her features, highlighting the curve of her cheek and the mesmerizing blue of her eyes. Each step they took felt like the start of a new adventure, a journey into uncharted territory full of endless possibilities.

"I never thought I'd find someone like you," Riley admitted, her voice tinged with a vulnerability that caught her off guard. "Someone who just gets me, who makes me feel alive in ways I never knew I could."

Morgan stopped, turning to face Riley. Her expression softened, a tender smile gracing her lips. "I know exactly what you mean, Riley. It's like everything in my life has led me to this moment, to you."

They stood there, lost in each other's gaze, the world around them fading into a kaleidoscope of colors and sensations. The air between them hummed with an electric current, a palpable energy that pulled them closer, like two puzzle pieces finally fitting together.

Riley and Morgan enrolled along the cliff edge path, admiring the pinks and purples of the sunsetting over the vast expanse of the ocean stretching out before them. The salty breeze whipped through their hair, carrying with it the promise of new beginnings and untold adventures.

Riley slipped her arm around Morgan's waist, pulling her close. In that moment, she knew that whatever challenges lay ahead, whatever obstacles they might face, they would face them together. Their love, still new yet undeniably strong, would be their guiding light, their anchor in the storm.

* * *

The twinkling lights overhead bathed the bustling reunion party in a soft, enchanting glow as Riley and Morgan stepped onto the patio. Laughter and chatter filled the balmy evening air, blending seamlessly with the gentle melodies floating from discreet speakers. Riley drew in a deep breath, savoring the heady scent of honeysuckle and freshly mown grass that enveloped her.

Morgan's fingertips grazed the small of Riley's back, a delicate touch that sent delicious shivers cascading along her spine. Even after all this time, Morgan's effect on her remained as powerful as ever. Riley turned, her emerald eyes meeting Morgan's intense sapphire gaze. An unspoken understanding flowed between them, an acknowledgment of the intricate history they'd navigated to reach this point.

Weaving through the crowd, exchanging nods with old classmates, Riley couldn't shake the nagging sense of unease. The past had an uncanny knack for resurfacing when least expected, and the weight of unresolved tensions hung thick in the air.

"Well, well, if it isn't Riley Thompson and Morgan

Hughes." A familiar voice sliced through the noise, dripping with saccharine venom. "The dynamic duo, reunited at last—for now—for how long?"

Riley's pulse quickened as she faced the speaker. Jessica Bradley stood before them, a knockout in a figure-hugging red dress that clung to her like a second skin. Her jet-black hair tumbled down her back in glossy waves, and her lush lips curved into a smile that didn't quite reach her cold, assessing eyes.

Six

MORGAN INHALED SHARPLY, her eyes widening at Jessica's loaded words. The tension between them was palpable, the reunion's laughter and chatter fading into the background. Riley's hand trembled slightly in hers, betraying the emotions bubbling beneath the surface.

"What exactly are you trying to say, Jessica?" Morgan asked, her voice steady despite the unease in her gut. Jessica's manicured fingers played with the stem of her wine glass, the crimson liquid swirling ominously.

"Oh, nothing really," Jessica replied, her voice laced with faux innocence. "It's just funny how the past never really stays buried, doesn't it?"

Riley's jaw tightened, her eyes flashing with a mixture of anger and trepidation. The weight of their shared history pressed down on them, memories of their high school rivalry threatening to resurface.

"That's ancient history," Riley said firmly, her free hand clenching into a fist. "What happened back then is irrelevant now."

Jessica's eyes narrowed, a smile that didn't reach her eyes playing on her lips. "Is it, though? Old habits have a way of sticking around."

Morgan's heart pounded as she watched the exchange, the tension crackling in the air. Riley's neck muscles tightened, her shoulders squaring as if preparing for a confrontation. It was a side of Riley she'd never witnessed before, a glimpse of the fierce protectiveness beneath her charming demeanor.

"We've grown up, Jessica," Morgan interjected, her voice calm despite the fear gnawing at her. "We're not the same people we were in high school."

Jessica's gaze snapped to Morgan, her eyes glinting with a dangerous intensity. "Haven't we, though? We all have our parts to play. The queen bee, the rebel, the outcast..." She paused, smirking. "And the secrets we keep."

A shiver ran down Morgan's spine at Jessica's words, the implication hanging heavily between them. She glanced at Riley, searching for a sign of the unease that mirrored her own, but found only steely resolve in the set of her jaw.

"If you're trying to get under our skin, Jessica, it's not going to work," Riley said, her voice low and even. "We're here to enjoy the reunion, not engage in your mind games."

Jessica laughed, the sound sharp and grating in the warm evening air. "Mind games? I'm just catching up with old friends."

"Friends?" Morgan echoed, the word leaving a bitter taste in her mouth. "Is that what you call it?"

She could feel the weight of Jessica's gaze, the intensity making her skin crawl. In the back of her mind, echoes of cruel laughter and whispers that had followed her through the halls of Crescent Bay High resurfaced.

But as she met Jessica's eyes, Morgan realized that the power they once held over her had diminished. The insecurities that had plagued her teenage years had been replaced by a quiet strength, a certainty in who she was and what she wanted.

"I think our definitions of friendship differ," Riley said, finding Morgan's hand and giving it a reassuring squeeze. "But that's fine. We're not here to dwell on the past."

Annoyance flashed in Jessica's eyes, her carefully crafted facade slipping for a moment. "No, I suppose you're not. You're here to pretend, to act like nothing ever happened between you."

Anger flared within Morgan at the accusation, the

insinuation that their newfound connection was merely an act. She opened her mouth to retort, but Riley beat her to it.

"What happened between us is none of your damn business, Jessica," she said, her voice steady despite the tension thrumming through her body. "We've moved on, and it's about time you did the same."

With those words, Riley gently tugged on Morgan's hand, leading her away from Jessica and the suffocating weight of her presence. As they walked, Morgan felt the tension slowly drain from her body, replaced by relief and gratitude. She marveled at the way Riley had stood up for them, at the strength and clarity in her voice as she'd spoken the words Morgan had been too afraid to say.

Around them, the reunion party continued in full swing, laughter and chatter filling the air as old classmates reunited and reminisced. But for Morgan, the world had narrowed down to the feeling of Riley's hand in hers, the warmth of her skin a comforting anchor in the chaos.

They found a quiet corner on the outskirts of the party, a small oasis away from prying eyes and curious whispers. Morgan leaned against the wall, her shoulder brushing Riley's as they stood side by side. For a moment, neither of them spoke, content to simply bask in each other's presence and the unspoken understanding that flowed between them.

Riley's thumb traced small, soothing circles on the back of Morgan's hand, the gentle touch sending shivers down her spine. Morgan's heart raced as she turned to face Riley, their eyes locking in a gaze that spoke volumes. In the dim light, Riley's green eyes sparkled with a mischievous glint, a playful smile tugging at the corners of her lips.

"Thank you," Morgan murmured, her voice barely above a whisper. "For what you said to Jessica. For being there for me."

Riley's smile softened, her free hand coming up to tuck a stray lock of hair behind Morgan's ear. The gesture was intimate, tender, and Morgan found herself leaning into the touch, craving more.

"I'll always be there for you, Morgan," Riley said, her voice low and sincere. "No matter what."

The words hung in the air between them, heavy with promise and unspoken emotion. Morgan's breath caught in her throat as Riley leaned in closer, their faces mere inches apart. She could feel the heat of Riley's body, the gentle puff of her breath against her skin, and for a moment, the rest of the world fell away.

But just as their lips were about to meet, a burst of laughter from a nearby group of partygoers shattered the moment, reminding them of where they were. Morgan pulled back reluctantly, her cheeks flushed and her heart racing. Riley's eyes sparkled with amusement and a hint of disappointment, but she didn't push, content to let the moment pass.

Instead, she laced their fingers together once more, giving Morgan's hand a gentle squeeze. "Come on," she said, tilting her head towards the party. "Let's go find some trouble to get into.

* * *

Riley leaned in close, her forehead gently touching Morgan's as a playful smile danced on her lips. "To new beginnings," she whispered, her warm breath tickling Morgan's skin.

Morgan grinned, her heart swelling with excitement for what the future held. "And to taking on whatever comes our way, side by side," she murmured, her eyes locked with Riley's, conveying the depth of her feelings.

"Together, we've got this," Riley affirmed, giving Morgan's hand a reassuring squeeze. "No matter what drama Jessica tries to stir up, she can't touch what we have."

"Damn straight," Morgan agreed, a mischievous glint in her eye. "We're a team now, and nothing's gonna break us apart."

Riley chuckled, her laughter mingling with the distant sounds of the party. "Look at us, getting all sappy and sentimental. Who would've thought?"

"Hey, I think we've earned the right to be a little cheesy, given our history," Morgan teased, bumping Riley's shoulder with her own.

"Fair point," Riley conceded, her smile softening. "I'm just glad we finally got our shit together and realized what we could be."

Morgan nodded, her heart full to bursting. "Me too, Riles. Me too."

* * *

Riley's hand tightened around Morgan's, a comforting anchor in the whirlwind of her thoughts. "Those rumors are just baseless gossip, Morgan," she said, her voice steady and sure. "What we have is real. That's the only truth that matters."

Morgan swallowed hard, wanting desperately to believe Riley's words, but the doubts still gnawed at her. "I know," she whispered, her eyes fixed on the horizon. "But what if people talk? What if they judge us for being together?"

Riley shifted closer, her warmth a soothing balm against the chill of the evening. "Let them talk," she said fiercely, her eyes blazing with conviction. "Their opinions don't define us or our love. We know what we have, and that's all that matters."

Morgan's heart swelled with love and gratitude. She

knew Riley was right, that their bond was stronger than any rumor or scandal. But still, the fear lingered. "I'm scared," she admitted, her voice trembling. "Scared of what people will think, of how they'll react. Scared of losing everything I've worked for."

Riley's grip tightened, her determination unwavering. "I'm scared too, Morgan. But we can't let fear control us, can't let it rob us of our happiness." She leaned in closer, her breath warm against Morgan's ear. "We have to be brave, to trust in our love. Because what we have is worth fighting for. Worth risking everything for."

Morgan let Riley's words wash over her, feeling their truth resonate in her soul. She knew, with sudden clarity, that Riley was right. Their love was a rare and precious gift, one that couldn't be denied or hidden. "You're right," she whispered, turning to face Riley, their faces inches apart. "We have to be brave. We have to trust in us."

Riley smiled, a slow, sweet curve of her lips that made Morgan's heart race. "Together, we can face anything," she murmured, her voice low and full of promise. "Together, we'll build a life that's ours, a love that lasts."

On the last evening of the reunion camp, Morgan and Riley sat on the beach away from the main group, watching the moon rise, hands entwined, hearts beating as one. The future was uncertain, but in that moment, with Riley by her side and the waves crashing in her ears,

Morgan knew they would find their way through, together. Always together.

Seven

THE SOFT CLINK of mugs on the worn table echoed through the cozy café. Riley's fingers traced her cup's rim, her heart pounding as she gazed at Morgan. The late afternoon sun caught glints of copper in Morgan's blonde hair and illuminated her pensive blue eyes.

Riley inhaled the rich scent of coffee and pastries. She straightened her shoulders, mustering her courage. "So," she began, her voice steady despite her nerves. "Tell me about this job offer you got that your need to talk to me about." She smiled, but tension tugged at her lips.

Morgan's hands tightened around her mug as she met Riley's gaze. A flicker of something unreadable crossed her features before vanishing. "It's an incredible opportunity," she said carefully. "A chance to work with a respected New York publishing house." Pride and excitement colored her tone, but hesitancy lingered beneath.

Riley nodded, ignoring the sinking feeling in her chest. The café's sounds faded as her mind raced. New York. A world away from Crescent Bay. A world without Morgan, without stolen glances, brushing fingers, and laughter under the stars. Riley swallowed hard.

"That sounds amazing," she managed, hoping her voice didn't betray her emotions. "You'd be brilliant there. They'd be lucky to have you.

Riley's hand twitched, yearning to reach for Morgan's. But she resisted, curling her fingers into her palm instead.

Morgan's eyes softened, a ghost of a smile on her lips. "Thank you, Riley. That means a lot." Her voice was warm, but tinged with something bittersweet.

Silence stretched between them, heavy with unspoken words and questions. Riley's heart ached. She knew what this job meant for Morgan's career and dreams. But selfishly, desperately, she wanted to beg her to stay, to choose them.

Outside, the sun descended, painting the sky in oranges and pinks. The fading light cast shadows across the table, over their hands and the cooling coffee.

Riley met Morgan's gaze, searching, seeking answers to unasked questions. In that moment, the world fell away, leaving only them, caught between hope and fear, love and uncertainty.

"I want nothing more than to support your dreams, Morgan," Riley said, her voice barely above a whisper. "But the thought of losing you, of not having you by my side..." Her words trailed off as a lump formed in her throat.

Morgan reached across the table, gently caressing Riley's cheek. The warmth of her touch sent a shiver down Riley's spine, igniting a familiar longing. "Riley, you could never lose me. No matter where I go, my heart will always belong to you."

Riley leaned into Morgan's touch, savoring the comforting scent of her skin. The café's soft lighting cast a warm glow on Morgan's features, highlighting the love and sincerity in her eyes. Riley's heart swelled with a bittersweet mix of adoration and fear.

"I know, but..." Riley paused, her voice cracking with emotion. "What if the distance is too much? What if we drift apart?" The words tasted bitter on her tongue, but she needed to voice her deepest fears.

Morgan's thumb gently wiped away the single tear that escaped Riley's eye. "We won't let that happen. We've faced challenges before, and we've always come out stronger. This is just another chapter in our story, Riley.

Morgan's grip tightened on Riley's hand, a steadying presence as they navigated the emotional storm. She met Riley's gaze, her voice soft but unwavering. "I know this is a lot to process, and I understand if you need time to wrap your head around it."

Riley's throat constricted, her heart racing as conflicting emotions battled within her. She wanted to be Morgan's rock, to support her unconditionally, but the fear of losing what they had was overwhelming. "I... I'm terrified, Morgan. Terrified of losing you, of our relationship falling apart."

Morgan's expression softened, a flicker of pain crossing her features. She leaned in, gently brushing a stray lock of hair from Riley's face, the tender gesture speaking volumes. "Riles, you could never lose me. No matter the distance, no matter what life throws at us, you will always have a piece of my heart."

Riley leaned into Morgan's touch, savoring the comfort it provided. When she opened her eyes, they glistened with unshed tears. "But what if it's not enough? What if the miles between us are too much, and we grow apart?"

Morgan's thumb gently wiped away the lone tear that escaped down Riley's cheek. "We're stronger than that, Riley. Our love is not something that can be broken by distance or time apart." Her voice was firm, a promise in the dimming light. "I love you, and that love will always lead me back to you, wherever this journey takes me."

Riley's heart swelled, a bittersweet mix of love and fear. Deep down, she knew Morgan was right. Their love had weathered storms before and emerged stronger. But the fear lingered, a nagging presence in the back of her mind.

She brought their joined hands to her lips, pressing a soft kiss to Morgan's knuckles. "I love you too, Morgan. More than anything. And I want you to follow your dreams, even if it means being apart for a while." The words were heavy, but she meant every one. "Just promise me one thing?"

Morgan searched Riley's face, a silent question in her eyes. "Anything," she breathed.

"Promise me that you'll come back to me, to Crescent Bay. That this will always be your home, no matter where your career takes you." Riley's voice wavered, thick with emotion, but her gaze held steady.

A tender smile spread across Morgan's face, like the first light of dawn breaking through the darkness. She brought their entwined hands to her lips, pressing a reverent kiss to the inside of Riley's wrist. "I promise, Riley. You are my home, my heart, my everything. And I will always find my way back to you, no matter what."

Riley's heart swelled at Morgan's promise, the sincerity in her voice easing her fears. She leaned in, their foreheads touching, their breaths mingling in the intimate space between them. The familiar scent of coffee and Morgan's perfume enveloped Riley, grounding her in the moment.

"I believe in you, Morgan," Riley whispered, her lips grazing Morgan's with each word. "I believe in us. We can make this work, no matter the distance or the challenges."

Morgan cupped Riley's cheek, her thumb tracing the delicate curve of her jaw. "I know we can, Riley. Our love is stronger than any obstacle. We'll find a way to balance our dreams and our relationship, together."

Riley nuzzled into Morgan's touch, savoring the warmth and comfort it provided. She placed a gentle kiss on Morgan's palm, a silent affirmation of their unbreakable bond. The soft glow of the café lights cast a warm halo around them, as if the universe itself was conspiring to keep them connected.

As they sat cocooned in their love, Riley's mind wandered to the future - to the late-night video calls, the heartfelt letters, and the joyful reunions that awaited them. She imagined Morgan, glowing with success, sharing her tales of the literary world, while Riley regaled her with stories of Crescent Bay's latest happenings.

A smile tugged at the corners of Riley's lips, a newfound sense of hope blossoming in her chest. She pulled back slightly, her eyes shimmering with unshed tears of joy and determination. "We've got this, Morgan. You and me, against the world."

Morgan returned her smile, her own eyes glistening with emotion. "Always, Riley. You and me, forever."

As the night deepened around them, Riley and

Morgan remained in their embrace, their love a steadfast anchor amidst the swirling tides of change. The path ahead may be uncertain, but with their hearts intertwined and their dreams aligned, they knew they could weather any storm, as long as they had each other.

The café's chatter faded into white noise as Riley and Morgan held each other's gaze, their connection drowning out the world around them. Morgan reached out, her fingers gently caressing Riley's cheek, sending a shiver of longing through her body. "I love you, Riley. More than I could ever put into words."

Riley leaned into Morgan's touch, savoring the warmth of her skin. Opening her eyes, she met Morgan's gaze with unwavering resolve. "I love you too, Morgan. Always and forever."

Hands clasped and hearts bare, Riley took a steadying breath. "Can we travel long-distance, meet up someplace, every chance we get?" she whispered, her mind searching for a way to bridge the impending gap between them. "Lots of little romantic getaways."

"Long-distance?" Morgan echoed, surprise flickering across her face.

"I know it won't be easy," Riley admitted, her thumb tracing circles on the back of Morgan's hand. "But I have faith in us, in what we share. We can visit each other, find ways to stay connected despite the miles."

A glimmer of hope ignited in Morgan's eyes as she

leaned in close, their faces inches apart. "You'd really do that? For us?"

Riley smiled softly, nodding. "I'd do anything for you, Morgan. You're my forever."

Morgan's lips curved into a smile, love and adoration radiating from every inch of her being. "Then let's make it work," she whispered, her voice thick with emotion. "No matter what it takes."

Hope blossomed in Morgan's heart as she considered Riley's proposal, a lifeline amidst the uncertainty threatening to swallow their future. She laced her fingers with Riley's, the warmth of their touch sending a spark through her veins.

"You're really willing to put in the effort?" Morgan asked, her voice barely audible. "To fight for us, even with the distance?"

Riley held Morgan's gaze, determination blazing in her green eyes. "Without a doubt. You're worth it, Morgan. What we have is worth fighting for, no matter how tough it gets."

Morgan's heart swelled with love and gratitude for the incredible woman before her. She knew the path ahead would be riddled with challenges and lonely nights, but the promise of a future with Riley made it all worthwhile.

As their conversation wound down, the weight of fear and uncertainty lifted, replaced by a tender intimacy that flowed between them. They sat in comfortable silence, hands intertwined, savoring the moment.

Riley leaned in, brushing a stray lock of hair behind Morgan's ear, the gentle touch sending a shiver down her spine. Their eyes locked, a silent promise of love and commitment passing between them.

Slowly, Riley closed the distance, her lips meeting Morgan's in a soft, lingering kiss. Morgan melted into the embrace, losing herself in the taste of Riley's lips, the scent of her perfume, the feeling of their bodies pressed together.

In that moment, the bustling café faded away, leaving only the two of them, their love, and the unbreakable bond they shared.

"I've been teased long enough. I can't wait to be alone with you any longer," Morgan said impatiently, tracing her fingertips along Riley's firm, rosy cheek.

Riley's eyes fluttered closed in response and Morgan repeated the action, gently rolling a sensitive ear lobe between her fingers. Riley bit her lip and they both felt the heat building between them.

"Come back to my place," Riley's voice was a whisper, beckoning Morgan closer.

"I need a shower," Morgan said. "I'm all smokey, sweaty, sandy and salty from the camping and hike. I want to be at my best to make love to you."

"We'll have to save water," Riley replied. "Shower with a friend."

* * *

Riley entered the shower, her glistening and nude figure irresistible to Morgan. Their lips met in a passionate embrace as Morgan's hands roamed over Riley's slippery skin.

The urgency between them was evident as Riley clutched onto Morgan, their bodies pressed against each other under the warm cascading water.

Their kisses were fervent, their bodies colliding against the walls of the stall. The sounds of their love making were muffled by the rush of water and their own moans.

As Morgan explored every inch of Riley's wetness with her hand, Riley's moans only fueled her desire. The electricity between them was undeniable, growing stronger as they shared this intimate moment.

It felt almost surreal how their bodies responded to each other, how eagerly they moved together in perfect harmony. As Morgan touched Riley's clit, their passion reached new heights and they lost themselves in the throes of pleasure.

When they were together like this, everything else faded away and their reality became the warmth of the water cascading down their bodies, their soft lips pressed against each other's, and the insatiable desire coursing through them. As Riley trailed her nails down Morgan's back and kissed her ear, she whispered "You're mine" before slipping two fingers into Morgan's tight entrance.

Morgan moaned and gasped, her hand gripping onto Riley tightly as she added a third finger and nibbled at her neck. Their bodies moved in perfect synchrony, Morgan's hips following Riley's lead as she teased her inner walls with her fingers. In this moment, Morgan was completely vulnerable to Riley and she reveled in every sensation.

With a swift movement, Riley shifted Morgan's weight and Morgan steadied herself by grasping the curtain rod. Riley's tongue flicked over Morgan's swollen clit slowly, savoring every sound and movement she made in response.

Morgan's gasps turned into moans as Riley continued to pleasure her with her mouth, and she grabbed onto Riley's hair for support. As Riley brought her closer to the edge, Morgan arched her back and let go completely.

Morgan_loved Riley in all her raw vulnerability, surrendering completely to their intense connection. She reveled in the sensations of her lover's full lips and tight grip on her hair.

Morgan worshipped Riley as she demanded and pleaded for more, promising to give her everything. Slowly and deliberately, she tasted and caressed Riley with her tongue, knowing exactly how to bring her pleasure.

As Riley's body convulsed beneath hers, Morgan felt a surge of pleasure build within her. She consumed her lover with fervor, pressing her against the wall as their passion intensified. And then, in a breathless moment, Riley whispered those three magical words, 'I love you,' that sent jolts straight to Morgan's core.

"Morgan," Riley gasped, and suddenly she was powerless. In this moment, she belonged solely to Riley, consumed by the need to hear her name on Riley's lips as she surrendered completely.

Morgan continued to lick Riley with fervor, reveling in the way her body responded. Riley moaned her name like a plea and cursed it in the same breath, but Morgan wasn't sure which she preferred. As Riley trembled and gripped her hair tightly, Morgan brought her to climax and they both succumbed to the overwhelming pleasure of their love for each other.

Watching Morgan pressed against the shower wall, Riley couldn't help but feel a sense of love and desire for her. As they came down from their intense physical connection, Riley pulled away and basked in the cooling water. She teased Morgan by tracing her lips with her fingers, tasting the remnants of their passion. The way Morgan gazed at her only heightened the thrill and excitement.

Standing up, Riley towered over Morgan's smaller frame. Despite the water losing its warmth, their eager exploration of each other's bodies continued. With every kiss, Morgan could taste herself on Riley's lips, igniting a fire within her that never failed to satisfy. As Morgan's hand trailed down Riley's back, sending shivers down her spine, a mischievous grin spread across her face.

Morgan murmured, "Did we use up all the hot water?"

Riley playfully teased, "We? You were the one taking a twenty-minute shower."

Her fingers traced over Morgan's skin, causing her to moan.

"I was just trying to wake up," she smirked before turning off the faucet.

Morgan pulled Riley close for another passionate kiss.

In that moment, all Morgan wanted was to make love to Riley against the shower wall. But instead, she surprised her by carrying her out of the shower and into the bedroom. Riley giggled as Morgan dropped her onto the wet sheets, still dripping from their steamy shower session.

"Looks like you're all wet now too," she playfully taunted.

Riley replied with a teasing grin, "I have legs, you know."

"I know. They're perfect for wrapping around me," Morgan replied, spreading Riley's legs open for her with ease.

Their kisses deepened and became more intense as

they moved onto the bed. Morgan's hands were on Riley's hips, guiding her towards her slick center. Riley's clit rubbed against Morgan's, driving them both wild with pleasure.

Despite Riley's overwhelming desire to feel Morgan against her, she held back. Instead, she reached for something from her nightstand.

"Do you have toys?" Morgan asked, her eyes gleaming bright with curiosity.

"How would you like to fuck me with a strap on?"

And that was all the confirmation Riley needed. She expertly strapped on the device, applied the lube, Riley handed her, before pushing it inside of Morgan, taking them both to new heights of ecstasy.

"Fuck," exclaimed Morgan.

"Say it again," Riley growled.

"Why?" Morgan asked.

"I like hearing you say it," Riley told her with a smirk.

"Love me completely, Morgan," Riley whispered. "I want to feel you inside me without any barriers - oh, my love."

Morgan entered her with one smooth motion, her body welcoming her and their legs entwined together. It was a beautiful and intense experience that made her pause for a moment, afraid of losing control.

"Is that how you like it?" She murmured.

"Yes," she whispered back, her voice catching in her throat. "Oh Morgan, you feel so amazing."

Even if she said it a million times, she would never tire of hearing those words from her lover. She loved her even more as they moved together, hitting all the right spots and eliciting moans and shudders from her.

"Tell me I belong to you," she pleaded, sinking deeper inside.

"You are mine," she responded, struggling to hold back her own moans.

Her breath hitched as she wrapped her legs around her waist, pulling her closer.

"Tell me I am yours," she begged, eyes half-lidded.

"I am yours," she answered without hesitation.

They move harder, faster. Their bodies are in sync, moving together like perfect machinery. But it's not just physical pleasure - it's an intense emotional connection between two women who love each other deeply.

She wants more. She needs more. She knows it will never be enough but she needs Morgan like she needs air. Their kisses are passionate and wild, their bodies joined as one.

Morgan pulls out and Riley rolls over, handing her a pillow. Morgan shoves it under her hips and slides back inside her again, the rhythm barely interrupted. Riley arches her back, on her forearms, her ankles wrapped around Morgan's legs.

Morgan delves her fingers deep within Riley and she sees stars, holding onto her tightly as her pleasure builds.

"Riley," Morgan whispers, and she knows she's close.

She kisses Riley's neck and she gasps, whispering "love me" into her ear. And that's all the signal Morgan needs.

She pulls out and they switch positions, with Riley wearing the strap on. She rides Morgan hard, their bodies moving together in ecstasy.

their bodies convulsed in unison, lost in the depths of their love for each other. Every touch, every movement was fueled by pure passion and desire.

Their fingers intertwined as they became one, their bodies merging in a union of love and desire. It was more than just physical pleasure, it was a deep connection between two women who were meant to be together. Riley moaned Morgan's name as Morgan whispered her love, over and over again. Their climaxes were cosmic explosions, drawing them in and making them lose control.

Afterwards, they lay together, holding hands and basking in the warmth of their love for each other. Riley admitted that she had missed Morgan while they were apart, and Morgan couldn't help but feel the same.

* * *

"Before you go..." Riley turned to Morgan with a mischievous smile. "I've been thinking... What if we took a little trip together now? Just the two of us, somewhere we can escape the world and focus on each other."

Morgan raised an eyebrow, intrigued. "Oh? And where did you have in mind?"

Riley's eyes sparkled with excitement. "Somewhere breathtaking, like a hidden beach or a cozy mountain cabin. A place where we can wake up to the sound of waves or birdsong and spend our days exploring, talking, and simply being together."

The idea sent a thrill through Morgan's body, the thought of stealing away with Riley, creating new memories and strengthening their bond. She squeezed Riley's hand, grinning. "That sounds perfect. Just you, me, and our own little slice of paradise."

Eight

PERCHED on a cliff overlooking Crescent Bay, Sea View Cottage offered the ultimate escape for lovers seeking a romantic getaway. Despite being listed for sale, the owners had agreed to rent it out to Riley and Morgan, who were in need of a more spacious and comfortable living space than Riley's cramped unit could provide at the moment.

The cottage was like a haven, with its panoramic views of the sparkling blue waters and the soothing sound of waves crashing against the shore. The sea breeze carried hints of salt and seaweed, reminding them of their close proximity to the ocean. As they settled in, they couldn't help but feel grateful for this little piece of paradise they had stumbled upon.

*　*　*

Making the most of the limited time they had together before Morgan would need to return to New York, Riley and Morgan moved together as one, their bodies finding a rhythm as natural as the crashing waves around them.

Riley kissed a trail down Morgan's neck, her tongue teasing along her collarbone and making Morgan shiver with desire. Morgan arched into Riley, their breasts pressed together, nipples hard and sensitive against each other's skin, sparks of pleasure igniting between them.

"Riley... fuck..." Morgan gasped, the words catching in her throat as the sensations overwhelmed her. Riley's fingers grew bolder, exploring and teasing, drawing moan after moan from Morgan's parted lips.

Their world narrowed to this moment, colors bursting behind their eyelids as their climaxes hit, washing over them in sync with the pounding surf. They clung to each other, riding out the waves of pleasure, their cries of ecstasy lost in the roar of the ocean.

As the intensity slowly ebbed, they held each other close, chests heaving and hearts racing. Riley rested her forehead against Morgan's, savoring the closeness, the way their bodies fit perfectly together. Morgan met her gaze, blue eyes filled with a swirl of emotions - desire, vulnerability, and a deep, unspoken connection.

"I never thought this would happen," Morgan whispered. "I was afraid to even hope..."

Riley captured her lips in a tender kiss, pouring her love and longing into the gentle caress. Pulling back, she smiled, her heart full to bursting. "I've wanted you for so long," Riley admitted softly. "I just didn't have the guts to say it out loud."

Morgan leaned into her touch, eyes fluttering closed for a moment. "Me too. But I was terrified of losing you, of fucking up our friendship."

Riley's heart ached at the raw honesty in Morgan's voice. She pulled her into a fierce hug, wanting to protect her from every fear and uncertainty. "You'll never lose me," Riley promised, her lips brushing Morgan's hair. "No matter what, I'm here for you. Always."

The setting sun bathed the beach in a warm, golden light as they held each other close, hearts beating as one. The future lay ahead, full of promise and possibility. Whatever challenges lay ahead, they would face them together, side by side, their bond unbreakable.

* * *

Riley pulled back slightly, her gaze locked on Morgan's face, taking in every cherished detail. The gentle slope of her cheek, the graceful curve of her brow, the inviting softness of her lips - each feature was seared into Riley's mind, an indelible portrait of the woman she had adored for what felt like a lifetime.

"What's on your mind?" Morgan asked quietly, her fingertips grazing the line of Riley's jaw, igniting a trail of sparks beneath her skin.

Riley melted into the touch, a smile tugging at the edges of her mouth. "I'm thinking about how incredibly fortunate I am," she said softly. "To have you here with me, to hold you close, to love you the way I do."

Morgan's breath hitched, her eyes glistening with the promise of tears. "I love you too," she breathed, her voice quavering with the weight of her emotions. "I've loved you for so long, Riley. Even when we were apart, even when I tried to fool myself into thinking I was better off without you, my heart always knew the truth. It's only ever been you."

Riley's heart swelled at the declaration, at the sheer depth of feeling behind those words. She had longed to hear them for so long, had fantasized about this very moment countless times, and now that it was finally happening, it almost felt too good to be true.

"I'm terrified," Morgan confessed, her words nearly lost amidst the gentle rustling of the waves. "Terrified of what this means for us, of how it could change everything between us."

Riley tightened her hold, resting her chin atop Morgan's head. "I know," she whispered. "I'm scared too.

But we'll navigate this together, just like we always have. One step at a time, one day at a time."

As the last traces of daylight surrendered to the encroaching night, Riley and Morgan stayed wrapped in each other's arms, their bodies fitting together like two pieces of a puzzle. The future was shrouded in uncertainty, but in that perfect moment, nothing else mattered. They had each other, and that was everything. More than everything.

Hand in hand, they watched a full moon rise, the town of Crescent Bay, with its prying eyes and wagging tongues, out of sight and mind. Tonight, they were simply two women in love, prepared to weather whatever storms life might send their way.

Nine

RILEY BURST through the front door, her heart pounding in her chest. Sam glanced up from her laptop, her brow furrowing as she took in Riley's tear-streaked face.

"Riley, what happened?" Sam asked, jumping to her feet.

Riley sucked in a shaky breath, the words tumbling out. "Morgan got a job promotion in New York and had to leave suddenly. I just got back from seeing her off at the airport. She's left Crescent Bay. I don't know when she'll be back."

Sam's eyes went wide. "Shit, Riley..."

"I can't lose her, Sam." Riley's voice broke, tears spilling down her cheeks. "I love her so fucking much. The thought of being without her... I can't breathe."

Sam crossed the room in a few quick steps, pulling Riley into a tight hug. Riley pressed her face into Sam's shoulder, her body shaking with sobs.

"Hey, it's okay," Sam soothed, rubbing Riley's back. "You're not going to lose her. Morgan loves you."

Riley pulled back, wiping at her tears. "But what if love isn't enough? What if she decides her career is more important than us?"

Sam shook her head, a small smile tugging at her lips. "Riley, I've seen you and Morgan together. What you have is special. She's not going to throw that away."

Riley chewed her lip, hope warring with fear. "You think so?"

"I know so." Sam squeezed Riley's shoulders, her eyes fierce. "But you have to fight for it. Tell Morgan how you feel."

Riley nodded, determination settling over her. "You're right. I have to fight for us."

She grabbed a pen and paper from the table, uncapping the pen with shaking hands. The words poured out of her, spilling her heart onto the page—their love, their dreams, their future together.

Riley wrote until her hand ached, then folded the letter, sealing it with a kiss. Morgan's perfume clung to the paper, sweet and familiar.

She turned to Sam, clutching the letter to her chest.

"I'm not going to post this. I'll get on a plane and personally deliver it. I'll tell her I'll follow her anywhere."

Sam grinned, her eyes shining with pride. "Go get your girl, Riley. Bring her home."

Riley smiled fiercely, snatching her keys and racing for the door. Hope soared in her heart, the future stretching before her, bright and full of promise. With Morgan by her side, anything was possible.

* * *

Riley paced back and forth in unfamiliar souloundings, gripping the letter to Morgan tightly. She took a few deep breaths, trying to calm her nerves as she went over what she wanted to say.

"Morgan, this job offer is a once-in-a-lifetime chance, and I would never want to hold you back. But what we have together is special, and I'm ready to fight for it. I love you more than anyone else in this world, and I truly believe we can make it work, no matter what challenges come our way."

She paused, imagining how Morgan might react when she saw Riley—here, in New York, Morgan's home and work base. Would she be surprised? Touched? Hesitant? Riley knew Morgan had a tendency to overthink and get lost in her doubts. But she also knew the depth of

Morgan's feelings, the way her eyes softened when they were together, the electricity in her touch.

Riley closed her eyes, picturing different scenarios. In one, Morgan embraced her tearfully, vowing to never leave her side. In another, Morgan hesitated, uncertain and weighing the risks of their relationship.

No matter what happened, Riley knew she had to take this chance, to put her heart on the line and trust in their love. With a surge of determination, she squared her shoulders and headed out the door.

As the sun dipped below the horizon, painting the sky in vibrant hues, Riley made her way through the unfamiliar streets of New York. She knew Morgan often found solace in the city library, a peaceful escape where she could lose herself in books.

Entering the enormous building, Riley was greeted by the comforting scent of old books. She wound her way through the stacks, until she found Morgan tucked away in a secluded corner, seated with a book in her lap.

For a moment, Riley simply stood there, taking in the sight of her. The soft light played across Morgan's delicate features, her blonde hair framing her face, and her slender fingers delicately turning the pages.

Then Morgan glanced up, her blue eyes widening as they met Riley's gaze. Riley's heart skipped a beat, a rush of love and longing washing over her. She stepped forward, the letter trembling slightly in her hand, ready to bare her soul to the woman she loved more than life itself.

Riley drew in a deep breath, her heart pounding as she approached Morgan. The air between them crackled with tension in the quiet library. She knelt before Morgan, her eyes shining with unshed tears as she took her hand.

"Morgan," she whispered, her voice trembling slightly. "I know we've been through a lot, and the future is uncertain. But one thing I know for sure is that I love you."

Morgan's breath hitched, the book forgotten as she stared at Riley, vulnerable and wide-eyed. Riley could see hope and fear warring in her gaze, unspoken questions hanging between them.

"I can't imagine my life without you," Riley continued, the words tumbling out. "You make me feel alive, push me to be better, and see me for who I really am. We've got challenges ahead, but I want to face them together. I want to build a future with you, no matter what it takes."

Riley tightened her grip on Morgan's hand, her thumb gently caressing her knuckles. The warmth of Morgan's skin bolstered her resolve.

"I'm here, Morgan. I'm not going anywhere. I want to fight for us because you're worth it. You're everything to me."

Tears welled up in Morgan's eyes, her lips parting as if to speak. Instead, she leaned forward, cupping Riley's face with her free hand. The feather-light touch sent shivers down Riley's spine.

"Riley," she breathed, her voice barely above a whisper. "I... I don't know what to say."

Riley could see the emotions warring in Morgan's eyes—love, fear, hesitation. She understood Morgan's past hurts and her fear of opening her heart again. But Riley was determined to show her that their love was different, strong enough to weather any storm.

"You don't have to say anything," Riley murmured, leaning into Morgan's touch. "Just know that I'm here, and I'm not going anywhere. I love you, Morgan. More than I ever thought possible."

Morgan's eyes fluttered closed, a single tear rolling down her cheek. Riley gently brushed it away with her fingers, lingering on the softness of her skin. In that moment, the world around them fell away, leaving only the two of them, lost in the depths of their love.

Morgan's eyes slowly opened, locking onto Riley's. The intensity of their connection hung heavy in the air, thick with unspoken emotions. Morgan's hand slid from Riley's cheek to the nape of her neck, fingers tangling in her soft hair.

"I'm scared, Riley," she whispered, her voice trembling slightly. "I'm scared of losing you, of not being enough, of the distance between us. What if we can't make it work?"

Riley's heart ached at Morgan's vulnerability. She

understood those fears all too well, having battled with them herself. But in that moment, with Morgan in her arms, Riley knew their love was worth fighting for.

"I'm scared too," Riley admitted, her voice soft but steady. "But I believe in us. We've already overcome so much, and we can get through this together."

Morgan's eyes searched Riley's, seeking reassurance. In the depths of Riley's gaze, she found it—unwavering love and fierce determination.

"Together," Morgan echoed, a small smile tugging at the corners of her lips. "I like the sound of that."

Riley grinned, the tension in her chest easing. She leaned forward, resting her forehead against Morgan's. The scent of her perfume, a subtle blend of vanilla and jasmine, enveloped Riley, making her head spin with desire.

"We'll find a way," Riley promised, her voice low and husky. "We'll figure out the logistics. But right now, all that matters is that we love each other. And that love... it's everything."

Morgan tilted her head, capturing Riley's lips in a soft, tender kiss. It spoke of love, commitment, and their unbreakable bond. Riley melted into it, her arms tightening around Morgan's waist.

When they finally parted, both breathless, Riley saw hope shining in Morgan's eyes—hope for a future together, filled with love and laughter.

"Let's do it," Morgan said.

Ten

"I'VE MISSED you so much, and we'd only been apart a few hours," Morgan said, her voice catching. "Your laugh, your smile, the way you make everything brighter just by being you."

Tears slid down Riley's cheeks, glistening in the soft glow of the moonlight. "I missed you too, Morgan. More than I can put into words."

Riley felt a glimmer of hope, a sense that they had taken the first step towards mending what had been broken.

"Come to my place—our place," she said, her heart in her throat. "Let's start this new chapter together."

"I'll be there with you," Morgan promised. "Always."

Together, hand in hand, they would find their way

back to each other, back to the love that had always been their constant, their guiding light.

* * *

For a year they commuted back and forth between Crescent Bay and New York every possible chance they could get, combining their separate careers in different locations and their romantic get-togethers at various retreats in-between the city and the bay.

Now, they were both at Crescent bay for another reunion. Morgan stood at the edge of the beach, her blonde hair tousled by the salty breeze as she stared out at the moonlit ocean. A mixture of hope and fear swirled within her, the weight of their complicated past heavy on her mind. She closed her eyes, taking a deep breath of the sea air to steady her racing thoughts.

The sound of footsteps crunching on the sand caught her attention. She turned to see Riley walking towards her, the moon casting a soft glow on her face. Their eyes locked, a wordless exchange passing between them.

Riley stopped in front of her, her green eyes filled with a depth of emotion. "I'm here," she said softly, her words nearly drowned out by the crashing waves. "And I'm not going anywhere this time."

Tears spilled down Morgan's cheeks as her composure

finally broke. She reached for Riley's hand, their fingers lacing together with a fierce intensity, a silent promise to never let go again. "I'm terrified," Morgan admitted, her voice shaking. "Terrified of losing you, of not being enough for you."

Riley tenderly wiped away the tears from Morgan's face, her touch gentle and reassuring. "We're in this together," she whispered, pressing her forehead against Morgan's. "Every fear, every challenge, we'll face them head-on. You and me."

Morgan melted into Riley's embrace, the warmth of their connection erasing the years of separation. In that moment, everything felt right, like they were exactly where they were meant to be.

"I love you," Morgan breathed, the words tumbling out like a long-held secret finally set free. "I've always loved you, even when I couldn't say it out loud."

A smile spread across Riley's face, her eyes shining with unshed tears. "I love you too," she murmured, pulling Morgan closer. "More than anything in this world."

They held each other tightly, their heartbeats falling into sync with the rhythm of the waves. The moonlight cast a ethereal glow over them, a silent witness to their love that had withstood the test of time.

Morgan lifted her head, her blue eyes meeting Riley's green ones. She leaned in, their lips meeting in a tender kiss that held the promise of a future together, of a love that would guide them through whatever lay ahead.

In that perfect moment, as the stars twinkled overhead and the ocean sang its eternal song, Morgan and Riley knew they had finally found their way back to each other. The path before them might be uncertain, but hand in hand, they were ready to face it all, their love a beacon in the darkness.

* * *

Another Crescent Bay reunion. Riley and Morgan never missed them now. They represented the wonderful moment when they reconnected.

The splendor of the ballroom dimmed as Riley Thompson's eyes locked onto Jessica Bradley, standing poised and confident across the room. Voices chattered around her, but Riley's attention sharpened, her pulse quickening with each stride toward her mark. The aroma of costly perfumes intermingled with the subtle saltiness clinging to her from Crescent Bay.

Her gown whispered against the marble as she approached, a subtle reminder of why she was here. Jessica's long, dark tresses flowed effortlessly over her shoulders, a picture of understated grace. Riley almost respected the woman's self-possession, if only for a second.

Riley's friends observed from the periphery, their faces a blend of worry and curiosity, but she couldn't let them distract her. Her heartbeat pounded in her ears, a relentless rhythm stoking her determination.

Each step ratcheted up the tension, the atmosphere growing thick and heavy. The crowd's murmur faded, replaced by the hammering in her chest. Her green eyes, normally sparkling with humor, now blazed with resolve. Tonight, she would face the shadows that had lurked for too long.

Riley rolled back her shoulders and pressed on, steeled for whatever came next. Jessica loomed like a dark sentry, commanding the attention of the partygoers as Riley neared. The crowd subtly parted, amplifying the importance of their impending clash, an electric current snapping in the air.

As Riley closed in, she caught the faint narrowing of Jessica's eyes, a tell only she could read. Jessica's lips twitched, equal parts challenge and entertainment, a tacit game set to begin.

Riley stopped before her, the air between them laden with their tangled history. Jessica's icy, appraising aura seemed to reach for her, but Riley stood firm, anchored by the comforting scents of Crescent Bay.

"Jessica," Riley started, her voice level despite the storm within. "I see you haven't lost your flair for dramatic entrances."

The delicate lace at her wrist grazed her skin—a tactile reminder of her purpose. She stood tall, tapping into the inner strength forged through trials.

"Always, Riley," Jessica answered, her words silky and goading. "But it's so much more fun when I have company in the game."

Riley held her stare unflinchingly, letting the quiet stretch. She refused to be drawn in by Jessica's ploys. Her composed exterior belied the fire stirring in her core.

"I outgrew games a long time ago," Riley shot back, the ghost of a smile on her lips. "I'm here for something that actually matters."

In that instant, she became a pillar of grace amid the ballroom's swirling bedlam. The low hum of chatter faded to nothing, all eyes riveted on the electric showdown—a display of integrity squaring off against cunning.

The ballroom fell silent as Riley faced off against Jessica, the tension between them palpable. Riley's unwavering stance spoke volumes about the depth of her love for Morgan, a love that needed no defense.

"Jessica, your attempts to sway me are pointless," Riley said, her voice steady despite her racing heart. "Morgan is my rock, my constant in the chaos you try to create."

Jessica's lips twisted into a smirk, ready to unleash her venom, but Riley's calm resolve remained unshakable. The onlookers watched with a mix of anticipation and concern, their eyes darting between the two women.

Morgan stood at the edge of the crowd, her blue eyes shining with a blend of pride and apprehension, surrounded by friends who offered their silent support.

"Love doesn't bow to your ridicule, Jessica," Riley continued, her words ringing clear. "It flourishes in the face of adversity, growing stronger with every challenge."

As Riley's declaration echoed through the ballroom, the weight of her words settled over the crowd. Jessica's composure faltered, and with a final scowl, she turned on her heel and stormed off, the rustle of her gown a fading whisper in the grand space.

Riley stood tall, a beacon of strength amidst the shifting sea of faces. Her friends gathered around her, their presence a protective shield against the lingering tensions. Amelia's knowing smile and Henry's warm embrace reinforced their unwavering solidarity.

"You did it, Riles," Henry said, his voice filled with pride. "You showed her what true courage looks like."

As the group huddled closer, the earlier strain melted away, replaced by a sense of unity that felt as comforting as a soft breeze from Crescent Bay. Lena's gentle touch on Riley's arm anchored her in the moment, a reminder of the unbreakable bonds they shared.

"Your love for Morgan is the guiding light, Riley," Lena said softly. "It's what gives us all strength."

The remnants of the confrontation slowly dissipated, overpowered by the collective support that enveloped

Riley. The love she shared with Morgan was the thread that wove them all together, a force that could weather any storm.

Marco's voice cut through the hum of the ballroom, steady and assuring. "We've got your back, Riley. No matter what anyone says, we stand with you."

Eleven

MORGAN'S FINGERS twitched against her wine glass, drawing everyone's attention. The room fell silent as they turned to her, sensing the weight of the moment. Her usually calm eyes now flickered with intensity as she stood, her posture straight but betraying a hint of nerves.

"Hey, can I say something?" Morgan's voice broke the stillness, barely louder than the sea breeze drifting through the cottage windows. It carried a tremor beneath her composed exterior.

Riley's laughter faded, her green eyes narrowing as she studied Morgan's face, searching for hidden undercurrents. The playful spark in her gaze shifted to keen alertness, her heart racing. The air thickened around them, heavy with the scent of night jasmine and an elusive hint of expectation.

The room held its breath, the bookshelves now silent witnesses to the unfolding scene. Shadows flickered across Morgan's features, cast by the candlelight, giving her an ethereal quality.

Riley shifted in her seat, the rustle of her dress amplified in the quiet. A gust of wind whispered secrets outside, and she wrapped her arms around herself, bracing against the unspoken tension.

Morgan's lips parted, ready to unleash what was brewing inside her. Riley found herself on the edge of her seat, anticipation coiling tight within her chest.

Morgan inhaled, candlelight casting shadows across her determined face. The silence stretched between them, vibrating with unspoken words. She leaned forward, her eyes locked onto Riley's.

"Riley," Morgan began, her voice a tremulous whisper carrying the weight of years away from Crescent Bay. "There's something I need to tell you, something that's been growing inside me."

Riley's expression transformed into one of confusion and intrigue. The teasing glint in her eyes dimmed, replaced by an intensity mirroring Morgan's gravity.

"Whenever I leave this town to work in New York, I never stop thinking about you," Morgan continued, her words spilling out. "The laughter we shared, those long walks on the beach, the way your smile made everything better… It was always you, Riley. You were the anchor I didn't know I needed."

As Morgan spoke, Riley's breath hitched. Her heart felt heavy in her chest. Surprise widened her eyes; realization dawned on her face as if seeing Morgan for the first time.

The air hummed with tension, thick with salt, jasmine, and yearning. Light and shadow played across Riley's face, highlighting the features Morgan knew by heart.

"Every success, every line I've written, felt empty without you," Morgan admitted, her voice breaking with emotion. "Will you marry me?"

Riley's hands trembled, her composure threatening to crumble. Morgan's raw confession resonated within her, stirring buried feelings. The room faded away, leaving only their intertwined pasts and possible future.

"Please, say something," Morgan pleaded, her gaze unwavering, searching Riley's eyes.

Anticipation settled over the room, wrapping everyone in the moment's gravity. A collective breath was held as Morgan's words reverberated through the charged space.

"Oh, yes!" Riley's eyes met Morgan's, the fading sunlight reflected in their depths. "Yes! Being here with you," she murmured, "feels like the culmination of every path I've ever taken."

Their friends' faces reflected a mix of emotions, illuminated by the soft twilight. Hands clenched, eyes shimmered with unshed tears - a tableau of joy, surprise, and heartfelt support. Their silence was a sacred pact, witnessing the unfolding vulnerability between two souls.

"Even with all the praise," Morgan continued softly, "it was your laughter I longed to hear, Riley."

"Your spirit," Morgan said, each syllable trembling, "is the compass that always leads me back home." Her blue eyes spilled over with sincerity, daring to hope as they met Riley's emotion-filled gaze.

The resonance of Morgan's words lingered, inviting those present to ponder the depth of a bond too profound for mere words.

As they embraced, the room grew contemplative. Friends marveled at the serendipity of the moment, acknowledging the beauty in the uncertainty that lay ahead. Love, they realized, was an uncharted journey filled with unexpected detours and delightful surprises.

Their fingers laced together, a wordless promise, marking the beginning of a new chapter in their story. The air around them shifted, charged with unspoken commitments and the comforting familiarity of their shared past.

In the stillness that followed, Riley and Morgan stood hand in hand, reconnecting with an intimacy that felt both essential and longed for. Morgan gently caressed

Riley's palm, their joined hands a haven amidst the lively gathering. The dancing candlelight cast enchanting shadows, deepening the intimacy between them.

Morgan paused, her voice unwavering when she responded, "And this is where I belong, because my soul recognizes its other half in you."

The distant cry of a seagull pierced the tranquility. Their friends resumed their conversations in hushed tones, respecting the significance of the moment, their figures softened by the waning light.

As night descended, Riley and Morgan remained united, a testament to the strength of their connection. They knew the future held its share of obstacles, but together they had discovered a wellspring of resilience.

With one last look at the night sky, now adorned with the first glimmering stars, they moved forward in unison, prepared for whatever challenges awaited them, their hearts and minds intertwined.

* * *

Morgan's eyes sparkled with a mix of surprise and delight as Riley's words sank in. "You're serious? You want me to move back here, with you?" A grin spread across her face, chasing away the shadows of doubt.

Riley reached out, tucking a stray lock of Morgan's hair behind her ear. "I've never been more serious about anything in my life. I love you, Morgan. I want to wake up next to you every morning, fall asleep in your arms every night. This town, it's a part of me, but so are you. We can make this work, together."

Morgan leaned into Riley's touch, her heart swelling with the promise of a future she hadn't dared to imagine. "I love you too, Riley. More than anything. And the thought of building a life here with you, it feels right. Like coming home."

Their lips met in a tender kiss, sealing the promise of a shared future. As they pulled apart, Morgan laughed softly. "I guess I better start packing, huh?"

Riley grinned, her eyes sparkling with mischief. "I might know a place you can stay in the meantime."

Their friends erupted into cheers, their voices filled with joy and excitement. Sam pulled them both into a tight hug, her eyes glistening with happy tears. "I'm so proud of you two. You're perfect for each other, and I can't wait to see what the future holds."

Ethan raised his glass, his smile wide and genuine. "To Riley and Morgan, and to love that knows no distance."

Lily clinked her glass against his, her eyes shining with warmth. "And to the stories yet to be written, the adventures yet to be had."

Ollie popped open another bottle of champagne, the sound punctuating the air like a promise. "To new beginnings and happy endings!"

As the bubbles flowed and laughter filled the room, Riley and Morgan held each other close, their hearts full to bursting. In the soft glow of the living room, surrounded by the love and support of their chosen family, they knew that whatever challenges lay ahead, they would face them together. Their love was a force to be reckoned with, as constant and enduring as the tides that shaped the shores of Crescent Bay.

Twelve

THE GLOW of the candles danced across Riley's tiny bed sitting room, cast a warm, intimate light that seemed to shut out the world beyond. Riley and Morgan sat close on the couch, their bodies angled towards each other, a sliver of space between them inviting whispered confessions. The scent of vanilla and sea salt lingered in the air, forever tying the room to memories of Crescent Bay.

Morgan's eyes wandered the room, taking in the weathered bookshelves stacked with well-loved novels and the hodgepodge of seashells adorning the mantel, each one a piece of Riley's life, her passions. A heavy silence settled over them, weighted with unspoken thoughts. They had been through so much together, trials and tender moments that had only brought them closer, even when they least expected it.

Riley turned to face Morgan, her green eyes holding a seriousness that spoke to the gravity of the moment. With a gentle touch, she reached out, her hand finding Morgan's in the dim light.

Their fingers intertwined, a wordless connection that anchored them, a promise and a declaration all in one. The simple gesture bridged the distance between them, pulling them into a shared space.

Morgan savored the warmth of Riley's hand, the strength in her gentle grasp. It was a touch imbued with meaning, a reflection of Riley herself—the charming entrepreneur with a laugh that could chase away the shadows, now offering comfort through her presence.

Their hands rested on the cushion between them, a lifeline amidst the memories and unspoken musings. Bathed in candlelight, surrounded by the pieces of Riley's past and the reality of Morgan's return, they found a silent language that spoke volumes about the love blossoming between them in the quiet of the evening.

The candles flickered, the shadows dancing, as she and Morgan sat close on the couch, fingers interlaced—a quiet testament to their connection. The distant whisper of Crescent Bay and the rhythm of the tide provided a soothing backdrop to the moment.

"Remember when you first met my book club?" Riley asked, a smile tugging at her lips, her eyes sparkling with nostalgia. "Lana practically claimed you as family right then and there."

Morgan laughed softly, the sound warm in the quiet room. "Yeah, she said, 'Anyone who can make Morgan smile like that is already one of us.'"

"And my brother," Riley added, her laughter laced with affection, "he always joked that I'd end up a crazy plant lady with a house full of surfboards. Said he's never seen me so... content, so complete."

A flicker of hesitation crossed Morgan's features. "Not everyone has been so supportive, though," she murmured, her mind drifting to the less enthusiastic reactions to their relationship.

"True," Riley acknowledged, her thumb tracing gentle circles on Morgan's hand. "My aunt's still convinced this is just a phase, something that'll disappear with the next tide."

"Phases don't build futures or homes," Morgan replied, her tone measured, as if weighing the uncertainty that threatened their peace.

A heavy silence fell between them, thick with unspoken fears. Riley turned to face Morgan, her expression sincere in the candlelight. "I know it's scary, the thought of diving into this, into us, when there's doubt lurking just outside our happiness."

Morgan's breath caught, trapped in the intensity of

Riley's gaze. "Sometimes it feels like we're on the edge of a cliff, and I can't tell if we're supposed to fly or fall."

"Then we'll jump together," Riley said, her voice steady and sure. "And if we fall, we'll fall into each other. And if we fly, we'll soar higher because we're together. My love for you isn't defined by anyone else's opinions or our own fears."

A swell of emotion surged through Morgan, a mix of love and fear, hope and hesitation. She looked into Riley's eyes, those green depths that seemed to hold the very essence of life. "I want to be brave for us, for what we could be."

"Bravery isn't about not being afraid, Morgan. It's about choosing to move forward even when you are." Riley's whisper held the weight of an eternal promise.

As the candlelight flickered, the night pressed against the windows, making the world beyond their cozy sanctuary feel both distant and imminent. The future stretched out before them like an uncharted ocean, but as Riley and Morgan held each other close, their shared determination became the guiding light leading them through the uncertainties ahead.

"We're in this together," Morgan said, her voice steadier than the racing of her heart.

"Every step of the way," Riley promised, sealing the vow with a kiss that tasted of hope and the exhilarating promise of what was to come.

The evening breeze drifted through the open window, carrying the salty scent of Crescent Bay. Riley's tiny home was a reflection of her vibrant spirit—warm and inviting. Seashells collected from sun-drenched days at the shore adorned the mantel, while paintings of stormy seas and serene harbors hung on the walls, echoing the ever-changing tides of Riley's eyes.

Morgan's fingers absently traced the pattern of the throw blanket draped over the couch, the soft texture soothing beneath her touch. She could almost hear the crackle of the fireplace from cozy winter nights, the flames warming the space just as Riley's laughter did now.

"Penny for your thoughts?" Riley asked, her voice gently pulling Morgan from her musings.

Morgan met Riley's gaze, taking in the life they were about to merge. "Just thinking about the practicalities," she admitted, a hint of nervousness in her tone. "Like where to put my books and what to do about my apartment in the city."

Riley's infectious smile lit up her face. "Well, your books will have a killer view of the bay." Her expression softened. "As for your apartment, we'll work it out together. I don't want you to give up anything you're not ready to let go of."

Morgan felt the knot of anxiety in her chest loosen slightly. "I know. It's just a big change."

"Hey," Riley said, reaching out to take Morgan's hand,

"we'll tackle it the same way we always do—one step at a time." Her words were a soothing anchor in the midst of uncertainty.

"You're right," Morgan breathed, drawing strength from Riley's touch. "One step at a time."

They dove into discussions about closet space and combining their distinct styles—how could they live together in such a small place?

Morgan's sleek minimalism and Riley's eclectic bohemian flair. They strategized about blending their lives, recognizing the importance of compromise and open communication. Each potential hurdle was approached with care and understanding, weaving the foundation of their shared future with threads of mutual respect and love.

Outside, the moon climbed higher, bathing Riley's sanctuary in a soft, silvery glow. Shadows danced across the room, hinting at the unwritten chapters of their lives that they were about to pen together.

* * *

Candlelight flickered across the living room, casting an intimate dance of shadows upon the walls. Riley's heartbeat thrummed in her chest, a rhythm that seemed to harmonize with the soft crash of the waves outside her Crescent Bay home. She turned to Morgan, the warmth in her green eyes reflecting the flames and the depth of her affection.

"Are you sure?" Morgan's voice was a whisper, laced with the weight of their shared future.

Riley responded not with words but with action, leaning in to capture Morgan's lips with her own. The kiss was a silent vow, a crescendo of all the unspoken promises and whispered dreams they had shared. It was passionate yet tender, a fusion of Riley's free spirit and Morgan's thoughtful soul. Their breaths mingled, and for a moment, time itself seemed suspended in the cocoon of their embrace.

As they parted, Morgan's blue eyes held a storm of emotions—hope, fear, excitement—all swirling in the ocean of her gaze. But it was the anchor of Riley's steady hand, still entwined with hers, that offered a safe harbor.

Riley pulled Morgan close, the press of their bodies a testament to the strength of their bond. They held each other tightly, two silhouettes framed by the glow of candlelight and the promise of dawn's approach. In this embrace, they found a sense of hope and unity, a sanctuary where the whispers of doubt were drowned out by the steady beat of their hearts.

"Whatever comes our way," Riley murmured into the quiet room, her voice a soft pledge in the darkness, "we face it together."

Morgan rested her head against Riley's shoulder,

allowing herself to be enveloped by the love and certainty radiating from her partner. "Together," she echoed, sealing their commitment to each other and to the life they would build in the quaint coastal town that had seen them grow and now welcomed them home.

The night deepened around them, the candles burned lower, but the light within them—a beacon of shared dreams for their future in Crescent Bay—remained undiminished. Riley and Morgan, united in heart and purpose, were ready to step into the unknown, fortified by love and the unwavering belief in their journey ahead.

Thirteen

THE SUN PEERED through the blinds as Riley stirred from her slumber, alone in bed. She could hear the shower running and knew Morgan, her lover, must have already woken up. With a smile on her face, Riley rose from the warm sheets and headed towards the bathroom. She watched Morgan's silhouette behind the frosted shower glass and couldn't resist joining her. The steam filled bathroom echoed with their moans and laughter as they explored each other's bodies under the hot water. Eventually, they had to break away to get ready for the day ahead, but not before leaving a trail of kisses and promising to continue their adventures later on.

"Do you have to go?" Riley teased, revealing different parts of her body.

Without hesitation, Morgan replied, "No." She couldn't resist any longer and pulled back the robe further, fully revealing Riley to her. With a seductive smile, Riley tilted her head back as Morgan's desire for her intensified. The magnetic pull between them never seemed to fade.

"Get dressed, Riley. I've something to show you," Morgan said.

"Something more important than us, now?" Riley grinned and looked from Morgan to the bed.

"Something about un, now, and forever," Morgan said.

* * *

The salty sea breeze mixed with the morning's lingering chill as Riley and Morgan strolled hand in hand along the Crescent Bay boardwalk. Waves crashed against the shore, their rhythm a calming backdrop to the seagulls' raucous cries above. The weathered planks creaked beneath their feet, a reminder of the countless others who had walked this path before them.

Riley glanced at Morgan, whose thoughtful gaze was fixed on the horizon where sky met sea. The breeze played with Riley's wavy brown hair, while Morgan's short blonde locks stayed neatly in place, framing her pensive expression.

They walked in easy silence until Sea View Cottage caught their eye.

"It's gorgeous, isn't it?" Riley said, her voice warm and inviting.

Morgan nodded, a soft smile on her lips. "It's home," she replied, her tone as gentle as the lapping waves.

Fogged windows hinted at the warmth inside, and the pair stepped toward it. The For Sale sign was gone.

"We can go inside," Morgan retrieved a key from her purse and opened the door, turning to invite Riley to cross the threshold first.

Riley was startled to be greeted by the comforting aroma of fresh coffee and pastries. Their friend, Sam was there, pottering about in the kitchen. They sat down together, a welcome haven, the outside world held at bay by the steaming mugs and quiet chatter.

***

After Sam left them, they sat by the window overlooking the sea, Riley and Morgan savored a breakfast Sam had cooked for them that felt more intimate than ordinary. Their hands brushed occasionally, fingers grazing with a delicate touch, as gentle as the morning dew on the café's window boxes.

"You've got to try the raspberry tart," Riley urged.

Morgan took a bite, and Riley watched, mesmerized,

as a slow smile spread across Morgan's face, reflecting the moment's sweet sincerity.

As they talked, their words became a tender exploration of their innermost selves. Morgan shared her dreams, her ambition peeking through her introspective nature. Riley listened attentively, her laughter bringing a lightness to the air between them.

"Thank you for this," Morgan said, her gratitude tinged with a hint of vulnerability, Sea View Cottage is our sanctuary, it is meant for us, don't you think?

"Being with you makes any place feel right," Riley responded, her honesty hanging in the air, charged with unspoken promises.

Their eyes met over the last sips of coffee, holding a gaze that communicated more than words ever could. It was a look that went beyond the surface, hinting at the depths of their affection.

"Your name is beside mine on the owner's papers," Morgan said.

"What!" The teaspoon fell from Riley's finger's with a clatter.

"Sea View Cottage is ours." Morgan grinned. "We'll go to town after breakfast so you can sign the paper work, your signature beside mine.

In that quaint cottage, perched on the cliff overlooking Crescent Bay, Riley and Morgan found themselves lost in the beautiful mystery of love, their hearts beating as one to the rhythm of an uncertain future.

※ ※ ※

The world beyond the wooden porch was a vast darkness, the stars mere pinpricks in the evergreen canopy. The waves splashed, leaves rustling and nocturnal creatures calling in the distance. Riley sat beside Morgan on the bench, the candlelight dancing across her wavy brown hair.

"The shadows were alive today," Riley said, her voice a soft harmony in the night. "Like the trees had secrets just for us."

Morgan turned to face her, short blonde hair glowing in the candlelight. Her blue eyes, normally pensive, now shimmered with unspoken feelings. "Nature understands," she whispered meaningfully. "It feels our heartbeats."

They had spent their days exploring their new home and its surrounding nature garden, hand in hand, laughter echoing through the woods. Each step on the cliff edge path had brought them closer, both physically and emotionally. Now, as evening fell around them, they found themselves at a crossroads of solitude and connection.

"Today, with every step, I felt like we were charting our future," Riley began, green eyes reflecting the flickering flames. "Making memories with every footprint." She reached out, fingertips grazing Morgan's, promising endless affection.

Morgan's breath hitched at the intimacy. "When you reach for me, Riley," she said, barely louder than the crackling wick, "it's like you're piecing me back together." She closed the gap, palm pressing into Riley's.

Silence wrapped around them, heavy with potential and yearning. Words tumbled out, private vows shared in their own sacred space. Morgan's heart raced as she opened up.

"Before you, the world was incomplete. With you, it's a blank canvas waiting for our colors." Morgan's words hung raw and honest in the air.

"And you, Morgan," Riley responded, her voice a gentle caress, "you've shown me that love isn't about coexisting, but about being essential to each other." Her thumb traced Morgan's hand, a touch filled with affection.

They stayed there, surrounded by the sounds and scents of the bay breeze, two souls intertwined by the weight of their journey. The candlelight cast their silhouettes against the cottage's wood panneling, a picture of love woven into the fabric of the universe.

In that instant, the world narrowed to the warmth of

their touch and the profundity of their promises. Riley and Morgan existed outside of time, enveloped in a love both timeless and new. A testament to the idea that even in the wild unknowns of life, two hearts could find home in each other.

Fourteen

THE SUN SHONE brightly over the lush rows of the Crescent Bay vineyard where Riley and Morgan exchanged vows in front of their friends.

They planned to honeymoon at home, by discovering more of Crescent bay. Riley and Morgan walked hand in hand between the grape trellises, the scent of rich earth and sweet, ripening fruit enveloping them. The air hummed with the rustling of leaves and distant conversations, but in the comfortable silence they shared, unspoken words and emotions seemed to dance between them.

"Here, try this," Riley said, offering Morgan a glass of deep red wine, its hue reminiscent of a breathtaking sunset. Morgan sipped the wine, savoring the complex, bold flavors that burst on her tongue. She met Riley's gaze, searching for that familiar glint in those playful green eyes, the subtle smile that hinted at untold secrets.

Riley watched, captivated, as Morgan enjoyed the wine, the sun casting a golden glow on her short blonde hair. There was something captivating about the way Morgan lost herself in the moment, eyes closed, fully immersed in the sensory experience—a reflection of the thoughtful way she approached life. Amid their lighthearted teasing about the wine's cherry and oak notes, Riley felt a tug of inexplicable longing, a desire as heady as the vineyard's most prized vintage.

As the afternoon slipped away, they wandered the winding path through the estate, their laughter carried on the gentle breeze. With each shared joke and giggle, they let their guards down, revealing the honest beauty of being vulnerable with each other. Beneath the endless sky, they were two hearts exploring the intricate dance of connection—a push and pull of nearness and space, of discovery and understanding.

* * *

The morning after their wedding, as dawn broke over the slumbering world, Riley guided a drowsy Morgan to a field where a hot air balloon waited, its vibrant colors a striking contrast against the awakening sky. The sun's first light painted the heavens in soft pinks and oranges, a breathtaking backdrop for their adventure.

"Surprise," Riley whispered, her voice gentle, not wanting to disrupt the magic of the moment.

Morgan's eyes sparkled with awe, her heart racing with anticipation. The balloon grew larger as it filled with hot air, a symbol of the limitless possibilities that lay ahead. Riley's hand found Morgan's, their fingers intertwining, a reassuring connection as they stepped into the basket. Their hearts beat as one, a wordless symphony in harmony with the rising balloon.

They rose gracefully, the earth below growing distant as they ascended into the morning sky. Bathed in the soft glow of the early light, they watched the world transform beneath them—houses becoming miniatures, roads turning into thin threads woven through the tapestry of the landscape.

"It's incredible," Riley said, her voice filled with wonder. "Everything seems so simple from up here, doesn't it?"

Morgan nodded, her gaze drawn to the horizon where the sun now reigned supreme, casting a golden light over the world below. As they climbed higher, the complexities of life seemed to fade away, leaving only the purity of their love, soaring in tandem with their airborne journey.

They drifted quietly, the occasional burst of the burner above punctuating the tranquil silence. Side by side, suspended between earth and sky, Riley and Morgan found themselves in a space where time seemed to stand still—a moment of perfect clarity, belonging to them alone.

As they began their descent, the shared intimacy of the experience lingered, a precious secret that bound them even closer. With feet back on solid ground, they embraced, the strength of their love a force that transcended any challenge. In that moment, they understood that their love, like the balloon that had carried them aloft, was a vessel for endless adventures, a promise of soaring to new heights, propelled by shared dreams and whispered devotions.